19   e has married her magic-lanterneer Beaumont, who is now a successful mill owner. But though she loves her husband and their children Ophelia and George, Hope misses her old days of roaming around in gentleman's clothes. As she throws herself into the suffragette cause, and Beaumont into his work, their marriage feels ever more unstable. Can they rekindle the old magic they once made together?

PATRICIA KEYSON

◆

LOVE AT WAR

Complete and Unabridged

LINFORD
Leicester

First published in Great Britain in 2014

First Linford Edition
published 2017

A catalogue record for this book is available
from the British Library.

ISBN 978–1–4448–3220–4

Published by
F. A. Thorpe (Publishing)
Anstey, Leicestershire

Set by Words & Graphics Ltd.
Anstey, Leicestershire
Printed and bound in Great Britain by
T. J. International Ltd., Padstow, Cornwall

This book is printed on acid-free paper

PART ONE

1

This was nothing like their honeymoon in Paris. That had been a truly magical journey for Hope. Her husband Beaumont had been her all-consuming passion then, and it had also been her first time in the capital. She caught her breath as she wondered what had happened to quell the excitement that had burned between them.

'You seem pensive, Hope. Tell me what you're thinking.' Beaumont leaned forward and took her hand.

'I was wondering if the children are all right,' lied Hope. She had no wish to talk intimately with him.

'Of course they will be,' her husband assured her. 'The maid will take good care of them, and the nanny will make sure they have plenty to occupy their time until our return.' He laughed as he added, 'They'll be getting up to all manner of mischief with us not there to keep an eye on them.'

'But you are *never* there,' objected Hope. 'All you think about is your woollen mill and your work.'

Beaumont dropped her hand as if it were a red-hot poker. He sat back in his chair and said nothing, his mouth a grim line.

Immediately, Hope was contrite. 'That was unfair of me,' she admitted. 'Let us concern ourselves with something more pleasant. I don't want an argument on our first evening here.' She looked around the restaurant. 'This reminds me of the gentlemen's club we visited in London before we were married. Do you remember?' Her voice bubbled with mirth as she recalled the incident.

'How could I forget that? You dressing as a man was a most bizarre experience.' Beaumont smiled at her and took her hand once more. 'We had adventures then, didn't we? What's happened to us, Hope?'

'We had the twins and then we settled

down to a more routine kind of life, I suppose.' Inwardly, she sighed. She didn't regret the children at all, but motherhood — and, indeed, married life — was not as she had expected. Everything had changed rapidly after their wedding.

'Now we're back in Paris, we must instil a little magic into our relationship once again,' said Beaumont. 'I've an outing planned for the morning which I think you will enjoy.'

The evening passed pleasantly, and Hope found herself looking forward to the next day as they climbed the stairs to their room on the second floor of the gloomy hotel.

With the door shut firmly behind them, Beaumont took his wife in his arms and murmured, 'I love you very much, Hope. I always have done, and I am sorry if I am neglectful in my duties as a father and a husband.'

'Duties!' Hope pulled away from him. 'Is that how you see me and the children?' She collapsed onto the bed. Her bottom lip trembled and she shivered involuntarily. This was not what she wanted, and as far as she was concerned, the sooner she returned home the better.

'Hope, I don't know what I can do to make recompense.' Beaumont lingered by the bed.

In truth, Hope had no idea either, but she felt nothing would be gained by furthering their conversation now. She kept quiet and feigned sleep.

During the small hours of the night, she roused herself, and on hearing Beaumont's soft gentle breathing, slipped from the bed and undressed. Unable to find her nightdress easily and not wanting to disturb her husband, she slid under the bedclothes and drifted off into a troubled sleep.

When she awoke the following morning, the shutters were open and sunshine was streaming into the room. Beaumont was sitting at the little ironwork table on the balcony. Hope knew she must stop feeling angry about the circumstances which were keeping them apart, and make the most of this special time together. In spite of the distance which had grown between them, she loved Beaumont. She leisurely climbed out of bed and shrugged on a robe before going out into the sunshine and putting her hands on his shoulders. She kissed the top of his head and sat down next to him.

'Coffee?' he asked, holding up the jug.

'Yes, please. Are you going to tell me what this special outing is today?'

'We're going to the Louvre Museum. When we were here on honeymoon you were disappointed we didn't manage to see the *Mona Lisa*, so today that's what we are going to do. If you'd like to, of course.'

Hope sipped the coffee. 'It's a lovely idea. And tomorrow I have an excursion planned for you.'

'I wonder what that could be. A boat trip? The Moulin Rouge? No? Then tell me about this painting you are so keen to see. No one I have mentioned it to has ever heard of it.'

'It was painted by Leonardo da Vinci, and is well known in art circles. Mama

7

told me about it. I wonder if later in the week we could return, and I could set up my easel and make a copy of it.'

'Whatever you wish.' Beaumont took her hand and kissed it tenderly. 'All I want is for you to be happy. I love you as much as I did the day I asked you to marry me. In fact, I loved you with all my heart the very first time we met. We have our differences, that is natural. And I am sorry the mill takes up so much of my time. You must remember, it puts bread on the table for many families.'

'I don't want to argue today, but surely your manager is quite capable of dealing with the supervision of the mill. You yourself said it runs smoothly. And William Kenworthy has worked for you for years.'

'That is all true. The other truth is ... I like living in Yorkshire. I prefer the more relaxed way of life and the fresh air in the country.'

'We have parks in London.' Hope wished she didn't sound so petulant.

'We do. You know only too well that I spend a bigger proportion of my life in

London with you and the children than I do in Yorkshire. Because I want to be with the three of you.'

'It may sound churlish, but when you are away the time passes slowly, and when you are with us it flies by.'

'Then let us make the most of being together now.' Beaumont reached over and, clasping her hair, kissed her on the lips.

★   ★   ★

When they arrived at the Louvre Museum, Hope was excited at the thought of all the treasures within.

'I suppose you want to gaze upon the beautiful woman immediately, is that right?' asked Beaumont, taking Hope's arm and ushering her inside.

Hope shivered and held onto her husband, feeling a thrill from his touch and the anticipation of the day ahead. Excitement was something she'd missed lately. She shook her head. 'No. I shall leave it until later so I have something to look forward to.'

'Oh, Hope, I enjoy you when you're like this. Spontaneous and eager. Don't become dull like so many other women do.'

'As do men,' returned Hope, but she softened the words with a touch of her fingers upon his hand. 'The Salon Carré will be our goal after luncheon.'

As they toured the museum, Hope lost herself in another world. When her mama — who was a talented artist — and papa had returned from their grand tour, their daughter had eagerly listened to the descriptions of the treasures they had seen here. It was wonderful to be in the company of paintings, ceramics, and artefacts from ancient Greece and Persia. There was so much to see. She wondered what people would admire from the present time in years to come. In her experience, there was little to esteem. Perhaps that was what made her sullen: she would like to change some things, make a mark on the world. Having children was not enough!

'Hope, I think you should rest.' Beaumont was looking concerned. 'You're pale, and I don't want you fainting at my feet.'

'What you mean is, you're bored and want respite. Am I correct?'

Beaumont's eyes danced as he nodded his head. 'You know me so well, dear Hope. I prefer the practical side of life to the artistic.'

'I can't agree with you,' demurred Hope, wishing they were alone and she could kiss his cheek.

At last it was time to view her prize. Hope stood before the painting and tried to take in its magic. It was a lot smaller than she'd expected, but it was breathtaking. After contemplating it for some time, she turned to Beaumont. 'What do you think?' She was aware she was willing him to think it as beautiful as she did.

'It's a fine painting. Now, what shall we view next?' He turned and looked around the room.

'Beaumont,' admonished Hope, 'how can you dismiss this picture after a mere

11

few minutes? Don't you think the subject is beautiful?'

He put his head on one side and scrutinised the canvas before him. 'Not particularly, no. Certainly not as beautiful as my dear wife.' He smiled at Hope, who couldn't help feeling flattered by his remarks.

'Very well, Beaumont, as you are being congenial, I will allow you to take me back to the hotel. As long as you promise to return here and let me paint *La Joconde*.'

'I am always congenial, Hope,' laughed Beaumont. 'And I'm delighted your French has improved since our honeymoon. What does *La Joconde* mean?'

'It means 'happy' in French! It's also a pun on the sitter's last name, which was Giocondo.'

'Sometimes you astonish me, Hope.'

★   ★   ★

The early evening light rippled on the surface of the River Seine. Hope felt

12

content strolling along the bank, her arm through that of her husband.

'Well, my dear Hope, did the painting live up to your expectations?'

'She did.'

'I wish I shared your artistic nature.'

'In many ways, you do. Some of the slides you used for the magic lantern shows are works of art. It is a shame you so rarely put on your performances now.'

'Progress has been made, and magic lanterns aren't seen to be quite as magical as they once were. Just think of it — we now have moving pictures! We had good times, though, didn't we? And the children enjoy the impromptu magic lantern entertainments we put on.'

'Do you really suppose the children are all right? It is such a worry not knowing what they are doing, and George's health is still so fragile. Our hopes that he would become stronger as he grew have come to nothing. Twins, and yet so different, both physically and in their disposition.' Hope paused at a bench. 'Shall we rest awhile?'

They sat close together. Beaumont

broke the silence. 'Hope, I have been thinking …'

Hope giggled. 'That sounds ominous.'

'Please, Hope, this is serious. I will start again. I have been thinking for some time about our situation. I am finding it quite difficult to oversee the mill as I would like, and to enjoy family life to the full while living both in Yorkshire and in London. George's wellbeing is of great concern to me too. I think he would be healthier if we moved him to Yorkshire. He would grow strong walking on the moors and he would have fresh air to breathe.'

'All that dull stone, desolate moor and biting rain would make someone feel poorly, not well. I will *not* leave London. My life is there.'

'I do not wish to fall out with you. I simply ask that you give it some thought and do what is best for your family. Ophelia would be very happy. I can picture her striding across the moor, soaking up the atmosphere, then finding a cranny in some rocks to read her beloved

Brontë books. She would come home with purple-stained fingers from picking bilberries.'

Hope shook her head. 'She is perfectly happy in London. There is no need for me to consider your suggestion. I will not move to Yorkshire, and nor shall the children.'

'Very well. As you wish.'

Hope didn't look at him, but she could imagine the determined set of his mouth. How she wished he hadn't brought up this particular subject on their holiday, which had been intended to rekindle the magic of their relationship. She had no intention of changing her mind on the subject of where they lived, but she would do her best to ensure Beaumont had a wonderful time with her here in Paris.

She took his hand and squeezed it gently. 'Shall we return to the hotel for our meal? I believe your favourite dish is on the menu this evening. And then we could go dancing. What do you say?'

'I fear I am no longer a proficient dancer; but it will give me a chance to

15

hold you in my arms, and I will not forgo that opportunity.'

They returned to the hotel to change for dinner, and descended the stairway to the dining room, which was decked out with exquisitely starched white tablecloths and sparkling cutlery. Each table was adorned with a beautiful decoration of flowers.

'Aren't these delightful?' commented Hope as she leant forward to inhale the scent of the roses. 'Thank you for bringing me here, Beaumont.'

'The pleasure is mine. I can think of nothing more enjoyable than your company, Hope.'

Fearing he was about to discuss moving the family to Yorkshire, Hope said quickly, 'Except perhaps the turbot with caper sauce.'

'Ah, that sounds wonderful.' He rubbed his hands together as plates were put in front of them.

After enjoying soup of puréed vegetables, the turbot, and beef sirloin, they at last reached the pièce de résistance:

16

Crêpes Suzette. Hope marvelled at the flames flaring up from the pan; what a spectacle it was. She glanced at Beaumont, who was smiling. It would be perfect if he could recapture the passion he'd had for his magic lantern shows. When she'd first met him, he had seemed to have an enthusiasm which was missing now. He still gave a great deal of consideration to his workers, of course. And the library and adult place of learning in London, as well as at his mill in Yorkshire, were thriving. She would not dwell on his remarks about moving, and hoped he would forget about it — although Beaumont didn't let go of his notions easily.

Besides, Hope had her own reasons for not wanting to move north, which she knew were contentious. Her husband, whilst being a particularly fair-minded man, didn't like her involvement in the women's movement. London was the pivotal place to be if she were to achieve anything in her dedicated fight for women's suffrage: the right to vote.

'That was delicious, but you didn't appear to have much of an appetite.'

'I had my mind on other matters,' replied Hope. 'Don't forget, I have a surprise outing for you tomorrow.'

'As long as we spend the day together, I shall be completely happy.' Beaumont swallowed the remainder of his Sauternes. 'I shan't have coffee, will you?'

Hope shook her head. 'It's been a wonderful day, Beaumont. Thank you.'

Her husband wiped his mouth on his napkin and stood, offering her his arm. 'The day isn't over yet, Hope,' he said. 'You mentioned dancing. Shall we go through to the ballroom?'

'I fear we shall waddle around like ducks after all the food we've consumed,' giggled Hope. 'I don't mind abandoning it, especially as you will probably tread on my new shoes.'

Beaumont raised his eyebrows. 'I would do no such thing. But you are right,' he whispered, brushing the top of her head with his lips, 'perhaps we should go to our suite.'

18

★ ★ ★

The following morning, Hope woke
before Beaumont. She crept out of bed
and opened one of the shutters, which
allowed a shaft of sunlight to reach the
bed. Trying to make as little disturbance
as possible, she crawled back beside her
husband and, propping herself on one
elbow, gazed at him.

For a man of fifty, he could only be
described as handsome. Hope had noticed the looks other women gave him,
and how they would sometimes coquett-
ishly observe him with a flutter of their
eyelashes. It amused her, and if she told
him about it afterwards, he dismissed it
as nonsense.

She wound some of his dark hair round
her finger. He still kept it slightly long,
but his moustache and beard were always
neatly trimmed. Unable to resist, she
ran her hands across his shoulders and
down his arms, feeling the hardness of
his muscles.

'I've caught you now!' Beaumont grabbed her and pulled her tightly into his arms.

'I didn't mean to wake you! I just …'

'Shh, let me kiss you.'

When they drew apart, they gazed into each other's eyes. His dark brown irises were as mesmerising as ever, but now they held a hint of sensuality.

'I love you, Beaumont.'

He kissed her again. 'Now, perhaps we should dress. It would be a shame to waste our time in Paris. Unless you think staying in bed is not a waste of the day …'

By the time they descended to the hotel lobby, it was time for luncheon. Beaumont spent some time with the concierge discussing a suitable place to dine, and while he did so, Hope discreetly studied herself in one of the mirrors decorating the vestibule. She wasn't a vain woman, and devoted little time to her appearance — less so since she had become involved in the suffragette movement. Her outfit consisted of a plain skirt and dark jacket, with a white blouse and simple hat. Even she considered it dull. She had always taken good care of her hair, which, although not as abundantly rich as her mama's, looked healthy and glossy in spite of a few grey streaks among the sable tresses. Beaumont called her beautiful, but at best she thought of herself as quite pretty. She had grown plumper since having the children. Her clear green eyes were the only feature she felt able to admire in herself.

'I've ordered a carriage, Hope, are you ready?' Beaumont was at her side, ushering her out of the hotel.

'Are we in a hurry?' she asked.

'*Mais oui,*' he smiled. 'I'm hungry. We missed breakfast.'

Hope patted his midriff. 'I think you could do with missing a few more breakfasts. Where are we lunching?'

'It's a surprise.'

'Speaking of which, do you remember that I have a surprise for you today? But that will wait until this evening.'

'You're being most mysterious,' said Beaumont.

21

2

'What a charming place,' exclaimed Hope as Beaumont walked her around the Tuileries Garden. 'There is so much to look at. Oh, do you see those acrobats? How *can* they contort their bodies like that?'

'I thought you'd like it here. I read about it in the Baedeker Guide and planned a visit. I'm delighted you're enjoying yourself so much.'

'Dear Beaumont, we do belong together, don't we?' Hope felt overwhelmed with emotion as she clutched her husband's arm.

'Of course, my dearest Hope. We shall always be together, I promise you that. Nothing will part us. If we were not in a public place, I would embrace you and convince you of that fact.'

Hope held back her tears and tried to smile at the same time, which caused her to choke. Beaumont rushed to a lemonade stand and purchased a drink for her which she sipped.

'That's better,' she said, feeling her eyes water. 'Oh dear, what a fool I've made of myself. I am ashamed.'

'You have nothing to be ashamed of. Now, do you see what I see? Which would you prefer? A boat trip, or a ride on a donkey?'

'Do you remember the boat we went on with Mama? Doesn't that seem a long while ago? It was before we were married; indeed, before we ever contemplated marriage.' Hope recalled the time very well: it had been a wonderful day in Hyde Park, and Beaumont had been happy to sit in the boat while she and her mama rowed. Then there had been an exhilarating bicycle ride, followed by a picnic. However, it looked as if today might even surpass that idyllic day.

'You are wrong, Hope,' declared Beaumont. 'I *had* contemplated marriage to you, I just hadn't voiced it. As I said before, I loved you from the first time I saw you. I can tell you the exact moment you claimed my heart. You interrupted that smart dinner party given by your Aunt Constance to ask if the leftover food could be donated to the poor! How could anyone not fall in love with such impetuous goodness?'

Hope was at a loss for words. He remembered so much! Why couldn't he be as sympathetic to her newfound cause? On the verge of asking him why he resented her involvement with the suffragette movement, she was surprised when he took her hand and led her to the donkeys. 'This is what we shall do, Hope. A well-bred horse should probably be our preferred option, but let's enjoy ourselves. Up you get.'

Hope felt a little like a child as she oohed and aahed on the ride, pointing out some of the entertainments and stands selling toys. 'We must buy something for the children. Oh, look at those lovely wooden toys.'

Beaumont laughed. 'The children are too old for such trifles. But we will find something appropriate, I am sure.'

When Hope slid off the donkey's back, Beaumont was already by her side, and held out his arms to catch her. She gave him a hug, then gently pushed him away. 'I want to thank my donkey. I wish I had a treat for him.'

Having made a fuss of the animal, she was ready to search the stalls for something for their thirteen-year-old twins. 'These toys are delightful. Look how intricately carved this Noah's Ark is — and this train set, and these dolls … Oh, this dolls' house is charming!'

'It's not suitable. We must look and see what else is available.'

Hope took Beaumont's arm, and they strolled amongst the crowds, searching for the right gifts. 'Look at that — what is it?'

'It's a rather fine example of a praxinoscope.' Beaumont studied the device. 'I believe this one probably dates from the eighteen-sixties. See, if I spin the drum and you look at the mirrors, you'll see a small boy doing acrobatics.'

Hope gleefully did just that. 'It's similar to a magic lantern!'

Beaumont stopped the drum from spinning. 'Look inside, and you can see the strip of pictures. We can buy more picture strips to show different actions.'

'It's a perfect gift for George and Ophelia. They are fascinated by your magic lanterns, and will be delighted to receive this. It's prettily decorated, too, and with the little lamp on top, Ophelia will love it.'

'Then we must buy it.'

With the parcel carefully wrapped and tucked under Beaumont's arm, they continued to explore the gardens. Beaumont stopped to watch some small children playing marbles. 'Remember when ours were small? Such curious little people, learning new things almost every moment. They would have enjoyed siblings.'

Hope's heart sank. 'I am sorry, Beaumont, that you don't have the large family you desired, but we must think ourselves lucky. We have two wonderful children.'

'I am sorry for you too, my darling. The miscarriages were a time of great sadness. However, I feel that if you had taken the doctor's advice and rested, then maybe ...'

'Beaumont! Are you blaming me for my failure to carry a baby to term? How could you? I longed for those babies as much as you did. Do you know how many nights I've cried over their loss?' Half-submerged emotions bubbled to the surface as Hope remembered the abject misery she'd endured each time the doctor had been called just to tell her what she already knew: the baby inside her was dead. Beaumont was often not even there, having taken himself to Yorkshire. She'd tried to be understanding, but all she'd wanted was the comfort only he could bring to her — and he hadn't fulfilled that need. She struggled to breathe as her throat constricted, but she would not let herself give way to tears now.

'I do not wish to fall out with you, but I feel we should be as honest with each other about this as we are in every

27

other area of our lives. I have never told you before that I believe your failure to rest was a cause of at least one of the miscarriages.'

'I was looking after our children. Did you expect me to stop doing that?'

'No, I expected you to stop your work for the suffragettes. You spent all that time at meetings and handing out leaflets when you should have been at home with your feet up. You know I insisted on extra help for you and the children, but it didn't stop you going to the meetings, which was my intention.'

Hope could scarcely believe what she was hearing. So *this* was why he was against her involvement in the suffragette movement! It explained his attitude, but was almost more than she could bear. The whole trip to Paris was now tarnished by this conversation which she would never forget. But at least it explained why her husband resented the cause into which she'd passionately thrown herself. Thinking of the evening ahead, Hope was ashamed to admit to herself that her thoughts were a little spiteful. She'd planned a pleasant treat for Beaumont — but did he deserve it?

As if half-reading her mind, Beaumont asked, 'What pleasure do you have in store for me later, Hope?'

He smiled at her, and Hope realised he'd dismissed the subject and was already moving on to the evening. 'I have a headache now, and I'm not sure if I will be well enough to go ahead with the arrangements.' Her lips set into a sulky pout.

'Then we'll go back to the hotel and you shall rest. I'll be happy playing with the praxinoscope. You must not overtax yourself. I'll summon a carriage.'

In some ways he's so thoughtful, reflected Hope, *but in others, we are just at odds with each other.*

* * *

Hope lay on the bed and closed her eyes. In truth, she did have a headache, a throbbing which refused to let up. Should she give Beaumont the treat she'd promised, or not? With the question making her feel dizzy, she eventually fell into a light sleep, from which her husband eventually woke her.

'I've brought a cup of tea for you. Not easy to find in this place, I assure you.' Beaumont laughed as he placed the cup and saucer on the bedside table and perched next to her. 'How are you feeling, my darling?'

Hope struggled to an upright position and sipped her tea. It revived her considerably and she felt a lot more positive. Making up her mind rapidly, she said, 'I feel well enough to go out this evening, if that is agreeable with you.'

'You'll need to change, won't you? Your dress, although pretty, is very creased.'

Suppressing a sigh, Hope indulged in the comfort of a bath and changed into an indigo-hued silk dress which she'd bought especially for Paris. As she dabbed some rose scent on her wrists and neck, the smell suddenly evoked a memory of the time she'd dressed up as a man in order to sneak into one of Beaumont's magic lantern shows. As a single woman, she had been expected to go out only with a chaperone, which frustrated her dreadfully. She smiled at the thought of the adventurous times she'd had with Beaumont before he became her husband. It was strange how, after all these years, the memory should come to her now. And why was she thinking of good times with Beaumont as being in the past? She shivered, and found a cream lace shawl which she put around her shoulders before announcing that she was ready to leave.

Beaumont took her hands in his and kissed her neck. 'You do smell good. Rose perfume? Charming. I am looking forward to our evening, Hope. Where are we going?'

'It's a surprise,' she said.

'Then how can I instruct the carriage driver as to the address?'

'You can't,' replied Hope, 'but I can.'

'You've always been very forward. I used to admire it in you.'

'And now?' Hope tried to restrain her resentment as Beaumont turned away.

She approached the concierge and told him where they wanted to go. Returning to Beaumont's side, she took his arm, wishing fleetingly that she'd cancelled the evening and remained in bed. Another few days to endure Paris. Then she remembered her forthcoming visit to the Louvre Museum, and her lips turned upwards into a smile.

'How pretty you are still, Hope,' said Beaumont. 'For a woman of forty-one, you have a freshness about you which is usually confined to the young.'

'Thank you, Beaumont. We should go now.' Hope was pleased with Beaumont's compliments, and felt her grumpiness dissipate. They would have a wonderful evening, she was sure.

★   ★   ★

Sitting in the darkness of the cinema, Hope put her arm through her husband's and moved closer to him. She wondered what would unfold before them.

Beaumont was silent, and she stole a

32

sideways look at him. A smile played on his lips, but there was nothing else about him to indicate whether he was enjoying the motion picture or not. Hope didn't pay a lot of attention to the film as a rabble of butterflies were dancing in her insides.

Suddenly, Hope felt Beaumont squeeze her arm, and as she looked at him, a wide smile lit his face. She couldn't wait until the film was finished and she could hear his opinion. When he'd presented his own magic lantern shows, he'd had an enthusiasm and satisfaction which he seemed to lack now that the moving pictures had taken over.

Hope was pleasantly surprised and relieved at the content of the film, which involved an emperor being pampered, and several magnificent lions chasing people. There had only been the one film showing, so there had been no choice.

At the end, they left the theatre. Hope pulled her shawl tightly around herself, glad she'd brought it with her. Beaumont didn't speak, just took her arm, and they walked along, stopping at the crossroads while Beaumont looked about him. 'Which way shall we go?' he asked.

'I don't mind,' said Hope, shrugging her shoulders, wondering what was on his mind.

They continued walking until Beaumont pulled her into an *estaminet*. He ordered two cups of coffee and gestured for them to sit at a table near the window.

Unable to contain herself any longer, Hope burst out, 'Well, Beaumont, don't keep me in suspense. What did you think of the picture show?'

'It was incredible, Hope.' His eyes were shining with enthusiasm. 'As you know, I stubbornly refused to embrace the moving pictures. Their birth has taken away an audience for my still images.'

Hope wondered if he'd admit to his pride being punctured. 'But did you enjoy the story?'

'*Roman Orgy*, was it called? I've no idea what it was about, although I found the title a little risqué, and was at first shocked that you chose it. However, I put aside the content and saw the skill of the moving-picture-makers. Thank you, Hope. You are thoughtful. I shall reconsider my magic lantern shows, perhaps.'

Hope sipped her coffee, wincing at its bitterness. Beaumont's reaction surprised her, but she was pleased he wasn't angry with her for taking him to the Gaumont picture house.

She reached across the table and squeezed his hand. 'I am going to be honest with you, Beaumont ...'

'As if you are ever anything but honest.' His eyes twinkled.

'I came to Paris hoping some of the magic of our early years of marriage would be rekindled, but there have been times when I have longed for the holiday to be over. We have almost insurmountable differences, but we must remember we share many ideals too. As you reminded me, we came together over our concern for the welfare of the hungry and the education of the unschooled. We have achieved many things together, Beaumont.'

'Indeed we have.'

'I know you would have liked more children, but I hadn't realised you blamed my suffragette activities for the loss of our babies. I don't believe that to be the case, but if that is what you think, then I can do nothing to change your opinion. I believe that I am getting beyond childbearing years, but there is no reason we shouldn't adopt a baby or child. There are many children needing a home.' She waited for Beaumont's response to her suggestion.

'You have been thinking a lot. I thought your mind was on the Roman Orgy!' Beaumont chuckled. 'Adopting a child or children is certainly something I would happily consider. But as to you being beyond childbearing years, I must disagree.'

'Very well. Let us contemplate adoption, and if meanwhile I become pregnant and carry the baby to term, we will be doubly blessed.' Hope felt sure that the holiday would now proceed happily, and that she and Beaumont would have plenty to discuss and be very cordial.

★ ★ ★

Hope felt exhilarated as they approached the Louvre Museum on the final day of their sojourn in Paris. Today, she would attempt to copy the wonderful da Vinci painting. Once Beaumont had helped set up her easel, he would take himself off on a walking tour of some of the lesser-known sights.

'What's this? What's going on?' Beaumont took hold of Hope's arm and steered her to the edge of the clamouring crowd. 'Excuse me, what's happening? If only our French was better, we might make some sense of this.'

'You English?' a man asked. 'Looks like she's been taken. *La Joconde*. She's gone.'

Hope gasped. 'The painting's been stolen? But surely the police are pursuing the thieves ...'

'Ha! It's been gone forty-eight hours, and they've only just noticed. Unbelievable, isn't it? The museum has been closed for investigations.'

'Beaumont, let us find somewhere to sit.' Hope led Beaumont away from the noise and bustle, down a side street to a quiet square where there was a low wall. They sat close together.

'I can't believe she's gone. Who could have done such a thing? Why? How? What will become of her? I feel both sad and cross. How is it that no one noticed?'

'I expect we shall find out. There will be an account in the newspapers. Many of the people in the crowd looked like reporters. She will certainly be better -known amongst the general public after this event. Too late for people to see her, though. We must feel blessed that we had the opportunity.'

In spite of the gravity of the situation, Hope giggled. 'You barely looked at her. You couldn't wait to be gone.'

'You know me too well, Hope. I am glad I had the chance to see her, though, and now we are part of history.'

'What do you mean?'

'We were in Paris when the *Mona Lisa* was stolen,' Beaumont said. 'What would you like to do now? We must make the most of our final day in the city.'

Feeling most disappointed at the

outcome of the day, Hope sighed. 'I don't mind, Beaumont. It's all one to me now. As long as I don't have to view the monstrous Eiffel Tower.'

'Oh, I was about to suggest we visit there, but I'd forgotten the outrage against its construction among artists and writers. I really don't see what's so monstrous about it.'

Not wanting to elaborate, or mention the letters she'd exchanged with fellow writers and artists, Hope changed the subject. 'Perhaps you will help me set up my easel here so I may paint the Louvre. It will be a reminder of this day.' She was pleased that they were playful with each other, and that the excitement had brought them closer together. 'Then I should like to go to the river. I'm sure I shall find something to paint there. Mama would like a picture of the Seine.'

'Very well, Hope.' Beaumont good-naturedly set up Hope's painting equipment and then left on his walk, promising to return in an hour. Hope nodded absently, her mind already on her painting.

When Beaumont returned, Hope had captured what she felt to be a passable likeness, and was pleased with the result.

'That's delightful, my darling. You really are an accomplished woman, you know.' He placed his hand lightly on her waist. 'Now, are you ready for me to move your equipment to the riverside?'

The sun glinted off the Seine as Hope, inspired by the Impressionists, painted her picture. Beaumont sat in a nearby café with a glass of claret.

At last, the watercolour was completed, and Hope was ready to return home. She beckoned her husband over and he packed up the apparatus, and they went back to the hotel to collect their luggage.

'It's been a good holiday, Beaumont. Thank you.' Hope reached up to kiss him and he responded eagerly, hugging her to him.

'I think it was a worthwhile break for both of us. It was short, but now we shall return home to Ophelia and George. I can't wait to see them.'

3

After a rough Channel crossing and a delayed train, Hope was relieved to be home in London. When she entered the house she was perplexed. She was sure she could hear her mama's and papa's voices. It must be tiredness that was affecting her. Then Mama came into the hallway and hugged her tightly. 'Hope, you must not be distressed, but Nanny Swift summoned us. She did the right thing. It's George ...'

'Where is he? What's happened?' Goosebumps rose on Hope's skin and her mother's voice seemed to come from far away. She mustn't faint, she told herself; not yet, anyway. 'Tell me, Mama. Where is he?' she repeated, her voice squeaking with anxiety.

'Calm down, Hope, he's in his room. He's a lot better now, but he was poorly enough for the doctor to attend.'

Hope didn't wait to hear any more. She mounted the stairs two at a time, cursing her heavy travelling clothes which hindered her. Outside George's room, she caught her breath and willed herself to be calm; it would not help her beloved son if he saw her in turmoil.

'George, my dear child.' Hope approached the bed where her son lay. He was coughing and wheezing. She hugged him gently and kissed his cheek. He smiled at her as she sat in the chair next to his bed. 'We had no idea you were poorly. We would have returned immediately had we known.'

'It's all right, Mama,' Ophelia said as she entered the room. 'Nanny has been here, and Grandmama and I have taken good care of him. See, I am here with his medicine and a drink to wash it down. Come along, George, let me help you sit up so that you can take this.'

Hope watched astounded as George did exactly what his sister told him, before heaving coughs wracked his body. Hope held his hand until the attack was over.

'Papa said to tell you he would be up to see George just as soon as he's spoken to Grandmama and Grandpapa about the symptoms and the nature of his illness. Although I could probably have explained it just as well. Doctor Murray says the illness will run its course, and then George will slowly regain his former health, such as it was.'

Hope was amazed by Ophelia's maturity. It felt as though she'd left a child and come back to find a young woman. However, her son seemed younger, lying in bed with his eyes closed, pale and silent.

'Where is Nanny Swift now? Shouldn't she be supervising the sick room?'

'She was sitting with George through the night, Mama. She has gone to have a short rest and change her clothes. She left me to look after him, but she will be back soon.' Ophelia put her arms round her mother's neck and kissed the top of her head. 'I will ring for Molly and we will ask her to bring you a nice cup of tea. You must be tired from travelling, and you have also received a shock. In fact, Mama, you should go and rest. George is well looked after, and he knows you are home safely, so will sleep better.'

'No, no, Ophelia, it's you who needs to rest. Go and find your papa and ask him for the gift we have brought for you and George. It will amuse you.'

'I'd prefer to stay here and entertain George when he's awake. I have been reading to him and making up stories for him. I believe he prefers the make-believe ones because he is usually the hero in them. He is brave and strong.'

He would like *to be brave and strong*, Hope thought; *but it is not to be.*

The door opened and Beaumont entered, closely followed by Molly.

'Poor child.' Beaumont stroked their son's forehead. 'He is very warm.'

'I will bathe him with a cool damp cloth,' said Ophelia, and immediately set to work, plunging a cloth into the washbowl and wringing it out before gently wiping her brother's forehead.

Beaumont raised his eyebrows at Hope,

who shrugged and said, 'I hear you have been busy, Ophelia, but we are home now and can care for George.'

'But I like to do it. I no longer wish to play with fripperies, I wish to have a purpose to my life. I believe I have found my calling.'

Beaumont spluttered and quickly pulled a handkerchief from his pocket and buried his face in it. Hope checked her daughter's reaction, but Ophelia merely shook her head before smoothing down the bedding.

Taking the responsibility, but not wanting to demean her daughter's nursing skills, Hope said, 'Beaumont, would you go and tell Mama that I shall be down shortly, please? I expect Molly will soon be here with the tea; and George will be tired, won't he, Ophelia?'

'Certainly, Mama. Sleep is a good medicine.' Ophelia looked serious as she cared for her brother, and Beaumont took the opportunity of dashing from the room, still clutching his handkerchief.

'Is Papa quite well? He seems to be

behaving oddly. Perhaps it's the journey.'

'I'm sure you're right, dear. You have done a magnificent job of looking after your brother. I am very proud of you. Proud of George as well for not creating a fuss. Has he been a good patient?'

For the first time since her return, Hope saw her daughter relax and smile. 'Yes, Mama, he has. But he says that I am bossy. I only have his welfare at heart.' She sighed and sat on the bed next to George.

'I know,' said the patient with a small smile. 'Thank you, Ophelia. You're a kind sister.' There was a pause as he coughed again. 'But I should like to see the present Mama and Papa brought.'

Molly came in with a tray of tea and put it on the table.

'Yes, you will,' said Hope, 'and when you are feeling better we shall tell you both about our holiday.'

Ophelia nodded and Hope felt she was being dismissed. What had happened to her daughter? This was not the young girl she had left. Hope cast her mind back to her own childhood and remembered the fun and laughter which had emanated from the household. She'd been an only child, but her parents, especially dear Mama, had encouraged her to laugh and enjoy herself. She was the daughter of an earl and a titled lady, but had had the freedom to pursue her interests. She did not feel bound by constraints then. She sighed as she wondered how she could feel so trapped now with one of the people who had encouraged her to be herself — her husband Beaumont.

As she brought her thoughts back to the present, she wondered if perhaps Ophelia was going through a phase: she was certainly being attentive to George; and, to Hope's surprise, he was letting her take over. Deciding to leave the two children together, she went downstairs and joined her husband and parents.

'I'm sorry you had to come home to bad news, Hope,' said Mama, hugging her close. 'George is much improved, and I must say Ophelia has impressed us all with her good sense.'

'Yes, she is quite changed. What was wrong with you, Beaumont? You seemed on the verge of hysteria before.'

'It was when she said she had found her calling. I would be perfectly happy were she to study medicine, but it was the seriousness with which she announced she no longer wished to play with fripperies and wished to have a purpose to her life which amused me. It seems like only yesterday when she was playing hospital with her dolls and bandaging their broken arms. Now she has a real patient.'

'We must take her seriously, Beaumont. It's not good to belittle someone's interests.' Hope turned to her mother. 'I am pleased you were sent for, and grateful that you came to look after George. How long have you and Papa been here?'

'Just a few days, darling. And we are delighted to help. We love our grandchildren dearly. They are a joy, but we hate to see George so afflicted. Is there no way to find a cure for him? His cough is relentless.'

'It is a real worry, but the doctors

are unable to discover a remedy. We simply have to look after him when he succumbs.'

'I know, darling, but have you given any thought to taking him to a spa somewhere? Switzerland, possibly?'

'Tosh! How can that make someone better? Whisky might!' Hope's father continued muttering until he was silenced by his wife's glare.

'I tend to agree with Papa,' Hope said.

'And I agree with your mama,' Beaumont said loudly, silencing everyone. 'Such a shame that Ilkley is no longer prominent as a spa town. A stay in Yorkshire would suit us.'

Hope knew Beaumont was bringing up the topic of Yorkshire and its potential health-giving qualities in order to persuade them of the merits of his plan. She could feel her anger mounting. Just at a time when they should be united for George's sake, he was bringing up one of the main disagreements between them.

Her mother seemed unaware of the friction developing. 'Maybe you *should* take him somewhere to recuperate, where the air is fresh and clear. It would do his chest good, don't you agree, Hope?'

'I couldn't agree with you more, Prudence.' Beaumont smiled. 'I have been trying to persuade Hope of the merits of moving our household to Yorkshire, but she is unwilling to leave her own interests behind. I feel sure George would benefit from the change.'

'What's this, Papa?' Ophelia had quietly entered the room.

'Ophelia! What about George? Have you left him alone?' Hope stood up, ready to rush back upstairs to her son.

'Of course not, Mama, Nanny is with him now. He is asleep. He needs the rest. But Papa, what were you saying about Yorkshire?' Ophelia went over to her father and held his hand.

'I simply think it would be best for the whole family to move to Yorkshire.'

'How exciting. When are we going? May we have a dog? Oh, Papa, we could have a pony!' Ophelia's face shone with excitement.

Beaumont laughed. 'That's more like my little girl! There are many things to discuss, Ophelia, but I gather from your reaction that you would like to live there. It's a possibility, that's all.'

Hope glared at him. It was quite wrong of him to mention this to anyone but herself until they had discussed it properly and come to an agreement. The trip to Paris felt like a long time ago.

'Have you had the opportunity to visit your sister, Herbert?' Beaumont asked his father-in-law.

'Yes, and I was very pleased to do so. She's getting quite frail now. Poor Constance.'

'I should like to see her soon, Papa,' declared Hope, who was very fond of her aunt.

'I know, my dear, and I also know you often call upon her. She corresponds with me, and spoke very affectionately of you when we visited. Hope, my darling, for now you have enough to occupy you here, and I won't have you feeling you should be torn in all directions.' Papa was using his tone which brooked no argument, and Hope nodded her assent.

'Very well. I expect you will want to see her again before you return to Surrey. Please do give her our love, and I have a present from Paris you and Mama could take to her.'

'You are very thoughtful, Hope,' said her mama. 'I'm sorry you came home to a drama in the household. We shall leave you and Beaumont to yourselves for a while. I shall look in on George. Ophelia, will you come with me?'

Ophelia gripped her father's hand as if torn between staying with her parents and going back to look after her brother. Then she released her grasp and said, 'I really *should* like George to be well.' Tears glittered in her dark brown eyes. Wisps of hair were escaping from the severe style she'd adopted. Her dark hair was as luxurious as her grandmama's, with just a hint of red; it looked beautiful when allowed to flow freely.

Hope wished her mama, papa, and Ophelia would stay in the room, as she didn't want to be alone with Beaumont just at that moment. Her temper was not under control.

After they had gone, Beaumont said, 'So, it seems a distinct possibility that we shall move to Yorkshire, doesn't it?' He smiled at Hope, seemingly oblivious to her fury.

She took a deep breath. 'Beaumont, you had no right to voice your opinion.'

'It is my house, can't I say what I like?' he replied, quietly. He sat in a chair by the window.

'It is my house, too, and the children's. And, no, you can't say things in front of the children — or my parents — which we haven't discussed.'

'We've discussed a move.' Beaumont looked her in the eye.

'But you know I am against it,' Hope threw herself into the chair opposite her husband. She fiddled with the material of her skirt.

'Are you telling me you're against taking George somewhere his health might benefit? I can't believe that of you, Hope.'

'Of course not, you know I would never do that. You are twisting my words and not being at all fair.' Hope knew she would have to be careful, or she would lose this argument. She stood up. 'I am tired, and have a headache starting. I shall go upstairs and lie down.'

'As you wish.' Beaumont stood and put a hand on Hope's arm. 'Let's not oppose each other. I love you, Hope.' He bent to kiss her cheek, but she dodged aside and stormed from the room.

4

Nanny was plumping up the pillows to enable George to sit up comfortably when Hope made her usual morning visit.

'You seem somewhat better today, George. Are you going to try to eat some of the porridge Nanny has brought for you?'

'I am, Mama.'

'I believe he has improved a good deal in the past few days since your return from Paris. Maybe it is having Papa and Mama home which has helped your recovery, young man?' Nanny abruptly turned away when Beaumont entered the room.

'Good morning. How are you today?' asked Beaumont.

With his mouth full of porridge, George was unable to answer. Hope kept silent too. Her relationship with her husband had worsened considerably since their return.

Nanny tidied a stray wisp of hair behind her ear. 'He's much better, much better.'

Hope was surprised to notice the colour in Nanny's cheeks as she spoke. Leaving her husband and Nanny to discuss George's health, she sat in the chair at the side of the bed and observed the way the young woman was behaving. Her manner seemed slightly secretive, although she had to admit that Beaumont seemed completely unaware of any potential impropriety, and was treating her as he would any other member of their staff. Now she came to think of it, Beaumont had interviewed the young woman. Hope had accepted her husband's recommendation to employ her without any hesitation, and here she was living with the family ... and perhaps enjoying Beaumont's company more than was proper.

She was an attractive, voluptuous young woman. Her upswept hair showed her features to their best advantage. Crystal-blue eyes were set in a long, elegant face; her delicate nose was perhaps her prettiest feature, thought Hope; and her lively mouth was usually smiling, but this morning she was somewhat lacking in humour.

As Beaumont was about to leave the room, Hope took a deep breath and said, 'I thought we might entertain George together this morning. It must be dreadfully dull for him, lying here all day long.'

'I have business to attend to, and I'm having lunch at my club. I am quite sure you are able to divert George without my help — unless you have a meeting to attend or leaflets to hand out. I will spend an hour with him this evening.' He didn't look back.

Hope felt like crying. This wasn't the man she had fallen in love with and married. What had happened to tear them apart like this? She would have to try and talk to him again about their differences, but for now she must amuse her son.

'I won't be gone long, George. You may have another visitor before I return. A man. You won't recognise him, but it's perfectly all right for him to call on you.' Now that she had started the game, she felt a little better, and almost skipped along to Beaumont's dressing room, where she helped herself to a suitable outfit before returning to her son.

Adopting a French accent, she said, ''Ello, I am Richard. I believe your mama told you I might pay you a visit.' Hope enjoyed the look of amazement on her son's face.

'Who are you? Mama said you would come and see me. Are you a relative?'

'I met your father many years ago. I 'elped 'im with 'is magic lantern shows, and we went to 'is club together. We 'ad tremendous fun.'

George looked hard at the man in front of him, his face scrunching up as he did so. Then a small smile appeared on his pale lips. 'You look like my mama.'

'Do I?' asked Hope, enchanted. Then she reverted to her normal voice and added, 'That's because I am.' The giggles that sprang from the young boy delighted her. 'Your father and I used to visit places together that only men were allowed to go. I was curious to see them; and back then, when Queen Victoria was on the throne, young women had to have a chaperone, and there was no one to go with me except my dear maid Edna.'

'Tell me about your adventures, Mama. They sound exciting. I wish I could have adventures and go out and see fascinating things.' His bottom lip trembled and Hope felt her heart shred.

As she started to recount her escapades, embellishing them to entertain George, Ophelia entered the room. Today, Hope noticed, her hair swirled about her shoulders, and she was wearing a dress with frills and flounces which made her look young and adorable. What a change from the solemn girl she had encountered on her return from Paris! If only she could give her children the freedom her parents had allowed her ... But George coughed violently whenever he was taken out, and Ophelia hated to go anywhere without her beloved brother.

'Who are you?' asked Ophelia, narrowing her eyes. 'I wasn't aware George had a visitor.'

'It's Mama,' laughed George. 'Doesn't she look funny dressed as a man? She's telling me about the adventures she and Papa had before we were born.'

Ophelia came closer and peered at Hope's face. 'Oh yes, I can see it's you now, Mama.' She smiled and perched on George's bed. 'May I listen to your stories as well, please?'

With her arms around her cherished children, Hope continued her tales until Nanny entered the room. Her smile soon turned sour as she said, 'I wasn't aware there was a visitor. Ophelia, you should have sent for me or your mama.'

The children laughed so hard that George went into a paroxysm of coughing and Ophelia nearly slipped off the bed.

Alarmed by the effect the scene was having on George, Hope said, 'It's all right, Nanny, I *am* their mama.'

A sharp intake of breath from Nanny incorporated not only surprise, but also disapproval. 'I see, my lady,' was all she said.

The next few minutes were spent

calming George. *It's a good job Beaumont isn't here*, thought Hope. She was sure he would have shared Nanny's disapproval. Then she found herself wondering what else he might have shared with Nanny. Why did she have this kind of thought nagging at her? There was no evidence of anything inappropriate between them at all. Florence had proved to be a good nanny for her children in the short time she'd been with them. At first, they'd all missed their old nanny who had retired to the seaside, but Nanny Swift had endeared herself to the children — *and* Beaumont, it appeared. Hope was less sure how *she* viewed her now.

She shook her head to get rid of the ridiculous idea that there was anything unfitting between Beaumont and the nanny. Her husband was the most upright of men, and remarkably principled — or, at least, he had been when she was close to him and knew him well.

★　★　★

Hope sat at her escritoire chewing the end of her fountain pen. It had been a while since she'd written in her diary, and with George having a nap and Ophelia out visiting with her grandparents, she had the opportunity to do just that.

It is such a long time since I have penned my thoughts, I barely know where to begin. Of course, I must begin with Beaumont. He seems so changed and we no longer have the same joy in life we once shared. There are so many disagreements, especially concerning my interest in the suffragette movement. He blames me for the death of our unborn babies. He always wished for a large family.

I thought he and I shared the same beliefs. It seems strange now when I remember him giving me a piece of the special Mappin and Webb suffragette jewellery one Christmas. How long ago was that? It must have been 1908, three years ago. I can't remember when I last wore it. The

pearl, amethyst and emerald stones
are beautiful. I try hard not to antag-
onise him. Deep down, I am sure he
believes that both men and women
should be able to vote.

Hope paused and scrabbled around
in one of the drawers until she found
the necklace. She held it in her hand.
He had teased her when she told him
the meaning of the colours — purple
for dignity, white for purity, and green
for hope, her name. She briefly tightened
her fist around the necklace and then
stuffed it back in the drawer.

I feel distraught that he thinks I
would jeopardise the health of our
children in any way. He thinks liv-
ing at Moorcliff Edge would benefit
George's health, so I am blamed for
his continuing poorliness.
  I could not tolerate living in
Yorkshire. It is such a bleak, miser-
able place compared to the pretty
countryside of Surrey where I grew

up. Whenever I go there it is raining or worse, there is fog, and the buildings are made of dark, dull stone. Beaumont likes to take long walks across the moors: miles of barren countryside — bracken, heather, sheep, and nothing more. How can anyone like such a place? It is beyond me.

Then there is the new nanny. Now that I think about it, he encouraged Nanny Bonnett to retire as soon as she raised the possibility. I wanted to persuade her to stay until the children no longer needed her. She would still have been young enough to enjoy time with her sister in Margate. But Beaumont was keen for her to make the move; and, of course, helped her financially. I do love him for that. So why am I uneasy about Nanny Swift's relationship with my husband? She seems uncomfortable in my presence, and especially so when Beaumont is present. What other reason could there possibly be than that something *inappropriate is taking place between them? Is it possible his principles have taken a tumble and he has succumbed to temptation because our relationship is so unstable? Well, I will not put up with it. I will insist that we sit down and talk about all our difficulties. In spite of everything, I love him with all my heart, and I do not wish to lose him.*

I will write no more. Now that I am decided on a course of action, I feel better.

★   ★   ★

'Hope, darling, I was wondering where you were,' said Prudence as Hope descended the stairs. 'Are you all right? You look worried.'

'I am fine, Mama. I was just writing in my diary. It seems a long time since I've done that. It's good to write things down; it sorts them out in one's mind.'

'You are right,' replied Prudence. 'Your papa and I would like to visit Constance once again before we return home tomorrow. Now that George is improving, we wondered if you would care to join us.'

It would be a pleasant distraction, and Hope responded with alacrity. 'Shall I ask Ophelia if she would care to accompany us? Nanny will be able to manage George, I'm sure.'

'She seems very capable, and a pleasant person. Do you like her?' probed Prudence.

'The children get on well with her,' replied Hope, tactfully avoiding the question, but she didn't miss the look of doubt which flitted across her mother's face.

Ophelia was delighted to be included in the invitation, and Constance seemed pleasantly surprised to see such a party arrive at her house. When the maid showed them in to the drawing room, Constance greeted them all warmly, but Hope noticed she gave Papa an extra-long hug. After a few minutes of adult conversation, Ophelia asked if she might go to the library.

'Of course you may,' said her great-aunt, with a smile. 'You take after your Great-Uncle Eustace. He loved sitting in the library and going on journeys with the books he read. Off you go, child. I'll get the maid to give you a call when tea is served.'

'Thank you. You are kind to me.' Ophelia's manners were exquisite, noted Hope. She looked so beautiful this afternoon with her hair freshly brushed, and wearing a print dress with a sash around the middle.

'She's a lovely child, Hope,' said Constance. 'She reminds me a lot of you when you were younger. It was such a pleasure to have you here with me when I was still in mourning for my beloved husband. I was overjoyed that you chose to marry Beaumont.' Her eyes shone as she spoke his name. 'He didn't start as a favourite of mine, but after he met you, he changed and became simply delightful.'

'I'm sure he would have joined us on our visit today, but he has business to attend to,' said Hope.

'He often calls on me; he's a thoughtful man. Now, let me ring for tea.'

That was a surprise to Hope. She had no idea that Beaumont called on Constance. There was no reason why he shouldn't, but he hadn't said anything about it to her. It seemed he was capable of secrets.

Ophelia joined them for tea, and they sat eating dainty lobster sandwiches and toasted crumpets oozing with butter.

'I shall have to undo my sash, Mama,' whispered Ophelia. 'But I really would like a piece of that orange and lemon cake. May I? Or is it being too greedy?'

'I think it will please your Great-Aunt Constance if you have some cake. It is not too greedy at all,' replied Hope. Her dear daughter had taken seriously the ethics instilled in her by herself and Beaumont about being aware of the poor people of the city. Even after all these years, they still put by leftover food for distribution to the needy. There was a lot of goodness in her husband; she wouldn't let him go. She didn't *want* to let him go.

* ★ ★

When Beaumont arrived home from his business engagements, Hope greeted him with a kiss on the cheek. 'I expect you're tired, my dear, but may we have a talk, please?'

'Of course, Hope. I would enjoy that, but I did promise to spend some time with George. I shall have something to eat and then see him. It's not that I put you second, but I promised.'

'Yes, I understand,' replied Hope. Her insides had been swirling with anticipation, and now Beaumont had deferred the confrontation, she had to suffer even longer.

She picked up a magazine and flicked through it, but all she could think of was Beaumont. Pacing the room, she checked the mantel clock, but its hands moved imperceptibly. Just as her nerves threatened to overwhelm her, Beaumont burst into the room.

'George is a lot better this evening. It's

a relief, I get very worried about him.' He poured himself a small whisky from the decanter on the sideboard, and sipped it before settling himself in an armchair by the fireplace. 'Ophelia told me about your visit to Constance. How is she?'

'Frail, but she was pleased to see us, I think,' replied Hope, not sure if she should mention Beaumont's visits to her aunt.

'Now, what is it you were looking so serious about earlier? You said you wanted to talk about something.'

Hope paced the room. 'You must remember, Beaumont, I love you and have only ever loved you. There is no other man who would be able to possess my heart the way you have.'

Beaumont grabbed her hand as she passed and pulled her towards him. Nestled in his lap, she wondered if she should spoil the moment by voicing her thoughts. But it must be now, or she would never do it.

Taking a deep breath, she said, 'I feel as though we have grown apart. You have kept too much to yourself. I had no idea you blamed me for losing our babies. It is a crushing accusation, and one I can hardly bear.' As Beaumont stroked her hair, wretchedness surfaced once again. 'You know that many working-class women work while they are with child. Their work is physically hard, yet they are able to carry their babies to term. I did nothing to make myself weak. I sat at meetings and handed out a few leaflets. It was nothing that could cause harm. If I had thought it would have made any difference, I would have stayed in bed for nine months!'

'I am sorry, Hope, but I cannot find any other reason on which to blame our loss.'

'Whatever you do, please don't blame me. If you hold this against me, then we are lost. We need to look to the future, a future together with our living children. We need to give them the best possible lives.'

Beaumont stared into his glass and was silent for a long while. Eventually, he whispered, 'You are right, as usual. I have been unfair. Will you forgive me for my accusation?'

Hope ploughed on, 'And now we should discuss the *Mona Lisa.*'

'Ah, it was you who stole her! You crept out in the night and have secreted her away somewhere so that you can look upon her whenever you wish.'

'Don't be silly! We felt differently about her. You were indifferent, and I fell in love with the painting. There is another woman I think we regard differently.'

'I am quite sure there are plenty of women we have different feelings about!'

'This is a woman in our employ: Nanny Swift.' How Hope now wished she hadn't started on the subject. If Beaumont admitted to infidelity, then her life would be ruined. If she accused him and he was innocent, their relationship could well be ruined.

'Oh, Nanny Swift. There are things concerning her I have not admitted to.'

Hope felt sick and faint. What was he about to tell her? She'd never be able to forgive him if he'd betrayed her with another woman.

'You are very intuitive. It's hard for me to divulge why I was keen for Nanny Bonnett to retire, and why I chose to take on Nanny Swift, who is so much younger and less experienced than other nannies we might have been able to employ.'

'So tell me, Beaumont, why *did* you take on such an attractive woman who possibly wasn't the best person to entrust with the care of our children?'

'Why do you say that? The children are very fond of Florence Swift, and she has a kindly way about her.'

Hope tensed, and realised she must summon all the tact she could. 'You are correct in what you say, Beaumont. I suppose I mean that she differs so much from Nanny Bonnett.' She got up from her husband's lap and sat in a chair facing him. 'Why is the subject of nannies awkward for you to talk about?'

'I can see you are not going to let this rest.' Beaumont put down his empty glass and sighed. 'Nanny Bonnett was having trouble with her eyesight, and was worried she couldn't look after the children properly, especially George. She also wanted to be with her sister. It's as simple as that. She approached me and asked to be released from her duties.'

'Why didn't she come to me?' asked Hope. 'She shouldn't have bothered you with household affairs.'

'Apparently you were often preoccupied or going out when she tried to speak with you.'

Beaumont didn't look her in the eye and Hope felt a tingle of guilt run through her. 'You mean I was engrossed in the movement, don't you?' Beaumont nodded. 'But that doesn't explain why you engaged Nanny Swift. As I recall, you did so with little reference to me,' she persisted.

'Hope, you don't need to know this, but I will tell you. At the club, I heard about an incident which shocked me. A young woman was being abused by her employer, and I took steps to save her, if you like.'

Stunned into silence, Hope sat forward, waiting for her husband to continue the tale. But he did not.

'Oh my goodness, the poor woman. Dear Beaumont, you are a very compassionate person. Why did she not just leave the employment?'

'Because she would have been homeless. I abhor cruelty, and I could not ignore this situation. In a way, I am pleased this secret is out, as Nanny still feels awkward about the episodes of mistreatment. But she is a good person, isn't she? You don't feel we should ask her to leave?'

'Of course not. She is welcome to stay with us for as long as she wishes.' Hope sat back in the chair as a wave of relief washed through her, closely followed by a feeling of revulsion towards whoever it was who had mistreated Nanny.

'And now I shall go upstairs. Will you join me?' Beaumont yawned widely and pulled himself out of his chair.

Hope cocked her head to one side. 'If you're sure you want to share a bed with an art thief, then yes, I *shall* join you.'

With delight, she saw a wide grin lighten his face as she added, 'Race you!'

The reconciled couple ran from the room, giggling like children.

5

'Mama, I shall miss you and Papa greatly. When shall we see you again? How can I thank you enough for coming to look after George?' Hope was breakfasting with her parents, but her enjoyment of the kippers and scrambled eggs was marred by her sadness at the prospect of the departure later that morning.

'It's our pleasure to be here, and we're glad George seems a bit better now. You and Nanny Swift will be able to nurse him back to good health,' said Prudence, biting into buttered toast.

'Ophelia has proved to be remarkable in her caring and capable attitude,' added Papa.

Hope nodded, her heart bursting with pride as she thought of her dear daughter. If only her son's health would improve, she would be the happiest woman alive.

Beaumont strode into the room and

helped himself to bacon and eggs from the many dishes on the sideboard. 'Herbert, if you and Prudence can be ready within the hour, I can give you a lift to the railway station in my automobile.'

'Beaumont, I should adore that,' replied Prudence, before her husband had time to open his mouth. 'I wish Herbert would get a motorcar, but he refuses to go whizzing around the countryside at ten miles an hour, don't you, dear?'

'I think we do well with our journeys abroad, Prudence. We both enjoy those.'

'I wish I could come to Surrey with you,' declared Hope.

'We have only just returned from Paris!' said Beaumont. 'Are you not pleased to be home?'

'Of course I am, and it's wonderful to be with the children, but I think I have travel in my blood.'

'Then something shall be arranged, my dear,' said Beaumont, leaning across the table and taking Hope's hand. He smiled at her as if they were the only two people in the room. 'I shall do anything for you. Just tell me your heart's desire — for travel, that is.'

'You are good to me, Beaumont. I shall get out the atlas, open it to a page, and stick my finger in.' Hope laughed at the thought. 'It will keep me amused after you have all deserted me. We can talk about it when you arrive back home.'

Prudence put her hand on Hope's arm and whispered, 'Darling, don't pester Beaumont. He has a busy day ahead of him, I have no doubt. Your impulsiveness hasn't lessened as you've grown older, has it?' She sipped the last of her tea and smiled at Beaumont. 'Please excuse me; I shall gather my things together and ring for someone to bring the bags downstairs. I shan't delay you.'

⋆ ⋆ ⋆

Knowing the truth about Nanny Swift, Hope wanted to make reparation for her unkind thoughts towards her. But when she entered George's room, she was surprised to find it empty. Then she heard laughter and voices coming from the play-room along the landing. She tiptoed up to the door and listened; George, Ophelia and Nanny were playing a game. She opened the door, and George looked up at her, beaming his bright smile. Hope's heart lifted. 'Am I interrupting your play? You all sound very happy.'

'George wanted to go out into the garden, Mama,' said Ophelia, 'but Nanny and I thought he should stay indoors for a little longer. Do you agree?'

'I am sure that whatever you and Nanny decide will be a good decision,' declared Hope. She realised she was not needed, so went to her room to write a letter.

Dear Edna,
How are you? And Thomas, and all your dear children?
I am very happy that you learned to read and write so that we can communicate even though we are living far apart. Beaumont has told me you have moved to a much nicer

cottage in the village. I will visit you next time I venture north. It may be a long time. You know how much I detest the place. I hear that Thomas is doing very well at the mill, and that he enjoys his work far more than when he was a delivery man.

I have been remembering our escapades. Poor George has been poorly again, and I dressed up as Richard to amuse him. You and I had fun together, but it seems such a long time ago when you were my dear maid. Now we are grown up with responsibilities.

I don't have a lady's maid at the present time, and will be interviewing shortly. If only I can find one as good as you! Please write to me when you can.
Your dear friend,
Hope

Hope folded the paper and placed it in an envelope before sealing it. She knew that many people — including her aunt's friend Lady Padstock — would frown on her friendship with her former maid, but she'd sooner be friends with Edna than many of the people she met in polite society.

Her thoughts were interrupted by raised voices and the sound of feet drumming up the stairs. Beaumont barged into the room.

'I've had the most dreadful news!' He waved a crumpled paper. 'This telegram just arrived.' He threw it on the escritoire in front of her, looking on the verge of unprecedented tears.

She smoothed out the paper and read it. 'Oh, my dear, that is quite awful. William Kenworthy, dead? It can't be true.'

Beaumont looked perplexed. 'I don't understand either. How could he have been killed in an accident at the mill? As the manager, he knew all the dangers. He was a very careful man.'

'You will find out soon enough. You must go at once. I know how much he meant to you, Beaumont, and it is a tragedy for his son.'

'Clarence will be devastated. As you know, his mother died in childbirth, so he has only ever had his father. You must come too. Clarence needs you.'

'But I hardly know him. I have met him only a few times. I have barely spoken to him.'

'I will be busy overseeing the funeral arrangements and investigating the cause of the accident. That boy is our responsibility now.'

'He must have other relatives.' Hope knew she was being selfish, but she wanted to stay in London with her own children. 'He must have someone.'

'There was no other family. We need to leave first thing tomorrow morning. Please have your bags ready, and tell the children where we are all going.'

'They are coming too?'

'Of course.'

If the children had remained in London, she would have been able to come home sooner. Now, she would have no excuse to return. Feeling compassion for Clarence, and with a heavy heart,

Hope rang for Molly.

After she had explained the situation to the maid, Hope said, 'You will need to let your family know of your departure north, won't you, Molly? I cannot tell you how long we shall be there.'

'I will send a message through the delivery boy, who should be here shortly. My brothers won't miss me as they are busy with their own families.'

'Very well. I will go and inform Nanny and the children of our impending departure, and then I should like you to help me with the packing. Nanny will see to the children's belongings.'

It crossed Hope's mind that Molly would make an efficient and practical lady's maid. She had been with the family for a long time without much advancement. It might be a good time to elevate her position. Perhaps she could ease her into the post when they arrived in Yorkshire.

Yorkshire! She was aghast at the thought of going to such an awful place. Even at this time of year, it would be cold

and unforgiving with its dark stone buildings and windy outcrops. The train would
take forever to travel the vast distance,
and she would be further away from her
mama and papa than ever. She must let
them know about Mr Kenworthy, and
Beaumont's instruction to take his family
north. There was so much to do. And
then there was the movement: she should
let them know she wouldn't be available
for the next several meetings. It was all
very inconvenient.

When Hope had explained to the children about their forthcoming journey to
Yorkshire, she was met with silence. Did
they dislike the thought of going north
as much as she did? Then Ophelia said,
'Poor Mr Kenworthy, of course we must
accompany Papa. And poor Clarence!
How will he manage on his own?'

'I like Clarence,' said George. 'He used
to take time to talk to me when I visited
his house with Papa.'

Hope was immediately contrite. How
could she have been so selfish as to put
her desires before the needs of a boy of

fifteen who had been orphaned in tragic circumstances? Her thoughts ran on — what if the machinery at Beaumont's mill was deficient in some way and he was responsible for the accident? With her mind going round in circles, she wasn't aware of Nanny Swift until she glanced up and saw her looking questioningly at her. 'I'm sorry, Nanny, did you say something? I am afraid I'm not concentrating properly.'

'I just wondered if I am to accompany you, my lady,' enquired the nanny.

'Of course,' replied Hope. She smiled. 'You are part of the family now, and we shall be delighted to have you with us. I'd forgotten you haven't visited our northern home.'

Nanny blushed prettily. 'The children and Mr Beaumont have spoken of it with affection. I look forward to seeing it.'

From then on, pandemonium ensued as Hope dashed around directing servants, deciding who should come to Moorcliff Edge with them, and who should stay behind to look after matters in the London house. It would be unfair to ask Beaumont's help, as he had his own matters to attend to. William Kenworthy had been his childhood friend as well as an astute mill manager. As far as Hope knew, there was no one who could replace him. As her thoughts came together, she realised that their sojourn in the north would not be a short one.

★　★　★

Beaumont couldn't stay at home with all the hubbub. He knew he should be helping prepare for the move and sorting out his papers, but he was devastated by William Kenworthy's death. He was soon at Constance's house.

'My dear Beaumont, take a seat. Some refreshment?' Constance asked.

'No, thank you, I haven't time. I called to tell you that we are moving to Yorkshire tomorrow.'

'That's very sudden. But why did you not send one of the servants to tell me the news? What is wrong, Beaumont? You

87

look terrible.'

'William Kenworthy, the man I rely on to run the mill when I am absent, is dead. There was an accident.' Beaumont could hardly endure thinking about his old friend being hurt. 'I know no details yet. I hope his death was quick and merciful. I wouldn't want him to have suffered.'

'Did he have family?'

'A son, Clarence, I have mentioned him. He's a little older than the twins.'

'And I have no doubt you will take responsibility for him.' Constance smiled at him.

'Of course — I am his godfather — but what can I offer him? He needs his father.' Beaumont clenched his fists. '*I* need William, too. He wasn't just an employee, he was a friend. We played together when we were children. We'd go up on the moors and pretend to be soldiers in the rocks. In spring, we took nets to the tarn and caught tadpoles. He grew up to be an intelligent and hardworking man. There are few people, Constance, one can rely on completely, but William was one.' It suddenly struck Beaumont that he should be saying these things to Hope, not her aunt. At one time, he had found it easy to talk to his wife, but lately it seemed as though they were unable to converse properly. He doubted it would be any easier in Yorkshire, as she would be feeling riled about the move.

Constance plucked at the sleeve of her gown. 'Might I make a suggestion? Hope has made it quite clear to me that she has no desire to leave London. She may be unhappy. Do not forget her in your efforts to care for Clarence and give William the funeral you feel he deserves. It is very true that there are few people one can rely on completely, but Hope is one of those people. You must give her the chance to support you during what will be a difficult time. This tragedy may bring you together.'

'You are right as always, dear Constance. I will endeavour to heed your advice. And now I must go and help with the preparations for the move.' He kissed Constance's cheek, and left the house feeling somewhat more able to face the future. With Hope by his side, surely he could deal with anything.

6

Whilst Hope made no secret of the fact that Yorkshire was not her ideal place to live, she *did* like Moorcliff Edge. It was a dark, imposing house, but Hope loved its cosy interior. For such a big place, it had a comforting intimacy. Over the years, she had added touches to the decor which Beaumont had accepted — more to keep her occupied than because he was in agreement, Hope had always thought. They had arrived after a long and wearying journey. She was longing to change her clothes and lie down, but she would make sure the children were settled first.

'Mama, shall I show Nanny Swift where our rooms are?' enquired Ophelia. The child looked pale and there were dark shadows under her eyes. She wished her daughter would take respite from caring for others.

'You and George go to your rooms,

darling, and I shall show Nanny to her room. I'll instruct Molly to bring a pot of tea to the nursery.'

Ophelia and George mounted the stairs, and Hope could see George was struggling. Poor lamb. How she wished again and again that something could be done to help him. She forced a smile and directed Nanny to follow her.

'What a pleasant room, my lady. I think I shall need a map to find my way around the house, it is vast! Oh, I beg your pardon, I spoke out of turn.' She blushed and fiddled with her luggage.

'It's all right, Florence. I do understand your concern about the house, but I'm sure you'll get used to it. The children will help.' She put her hand on the nanny's arm. 'I do prefer to be less formal. Perhaps you can drop my title when we are alone — what do you think?'

Nanny Swift nodded. Then she faced Hope and asked, 'Did Mr Beaumont tell you the circumstances of my engagement to the post of nanny to Ophelia and George?'

Hope was surprised at the question. 'He outlined your appalling story, yes.'

'Then I should like to offer you my profound gratitude for giving me a chance to work for such a close-knit and loving family.'

Unsure what to say or even think, Hope excused herself. She reflected on Florence's words. *Is that how we appear to others?* she wondered as she went to join the children.

'Mama, when shall we see Clarence?' asked George. He sat in a chair by the bed, leaning forward to ease his breathing.

'We must all recover from the journey. It seems to have taken your breath away, and you need to rest,' said Hope, stroking his back gently.

'I'm fed up with resting!' shouted George, shrugging away from her. He got up and went to the door. 'I'm going to find Clarence and tell him how sorry I am that his father is dead. It's the least I can do.'

'I'll come with you,' said Ophelia. 'I want to see him, too. And someone should go with George.'

Paying no heed to Hope's remonstrations, they left. They were growing up. Soon she would have little influence over them. She would have to make the most of their childhood years while she could. And now she would search out Beaumont and see if there was any way she could help him, rather than take the rest she had promised herself. The children had shown her that she should be thinking of others rather than herself.

She found him in the study, sitting at his desk, gazing into the full glass of whisky he was holding. Hope stood next to him and gently placed her hand on his shoulder. 'Beaumont, it is unlike you to drink so much. I wondered if I could help in any way.'

He put the glass on the desk and reached up to hold her hand. 'Drink is not the answer, I know that. I thought it might ease the pain. As for helping, there is nothing anyone can do. William is dead. I am unable to go to the mill and face the facts of the incident. I am afraid, Hope.

If his death is in any way my fault, how will I live?'

'It can't be your fault. You were hundreds of miles away in London.' Hope was indignant that her strong, fearless husband was so dispirited.

'It could be negligence. Suppose it is through my negligence that Clarence has lost his father?'

'This is not like you at all. First, we should find out exactly how William's death occurred. Not today. We are tired. Let us recover, then tomorrow morning I will come with you, and we will face whatever has to be faced together. Today we will spend some time with the children and have a quiet evening.' She wrapped her arms around him.

* * *

The children were subdued when their parents joined them. Ophelia said, 'George and I want to tell you about Clarence. Did Mama tell you we went to visit him?'

'She did, and I would like to know how he is bearing up.'

'He is being very brave, although George and I think he had been crying. His eyes were red. He looked very tired.'

'What will we do about him?' George asked.

'I have been giving Clarence a lot of thought. If he agrees, he must come to live with us,' Beaumont pronounced.

'That is wonderful, isn't it, Mama?' Ophelia looked at her mother.

Hope knew this was the right thing to do — but didn't Beaumont think he should have discussed it with her before announcing it to the children? It seemed not.

'Mama, Mama, it's a splendid idea, isn't it? It will be fun to have Clarence here to play with us.' George's enthusiasm resulted in a fit of coughing which saved Hope from responding.

'I am going to make sure he has everything he needs to make him happy.' Ophelia had found another cause for her caring nature to attend to. It appeared that the whole family approved of the plan. That being the case, Hope knew she must embrace the new member of her family. She thought back to Paris, where they'd discussed adopting a child. But Clarence was older than she had imagined the adopted child would be.

Scarcely aware of the animated conversation going on around her, Hope thought about Clarence. Why was she being unreceptive to him living with them? He was a young man of fifteen who wouldn't need a lot of looking after; and if he did, she felt sure Ophelia would bestow attention on him — whether he wanted it or not. Dear Ophelia, and dear George, also. They were such precious children. Yet she and Beaumont had longed for a bigger family. And here she was being presented with another child. Had her past heartbreaks hardened her? Perhaps Clarence would prove to be the catalyst she needed to revert to the gentler, kinder Hope, the one Beaumont fell in love with and married.

After a poor night's sleep, Hope and Beaumont breakfasted on tea and toast, neither of them possessing a great appetite or producing much conversation.

'Are you sure you still wish to accompany me to the mill, Hope?' Beaumont was uncharacteristically slumped in his chair.

'I promised, darling, and I think we should go together.' Hope wiped her mouth with a napkin and stood. 'I shall inform Florence of our plans.'

Beaumont gave the ghost of a smile. 'Florence? Is that what you call her now? She's in favour with you, then?'

'It's a nice name. And yes, I like her. I think we could be friends.'

'Like you and Edna, you mean?' He grabbed Hope's arm as she brushed past him. 'You're a good woman, Hope. I know I can rely on you completely.' He brought her hand to his lips and kissed it.

'How do you know that?' asked Hope, bending to kiss the top of his head.

'Constance told me!' laughed Beaumont. 'But I knew it before she said anything.'

'My darling, I never want to let you down. Now, let me go and get ready to face our ordeal.'

Deciding that a walk would do them good, Hope and Beaumont strode across the grounds of Moorcliff Edge and through the iron gate at the bottom of the gardens. It was a bright day, but already the faint chill of autumn wrapped around them as they walked hand in hand.

The mill came into view and Hope felt her husband's grip tighten. 'It's all right, Beaumont. I am here.'

'And I thank God for that,' he replied. Nevertheless, his steps faltered a little and he slowed his pace. Then he took a deep breath, raised his chin, let go of his wife's hand, and walked forward resolutely.

Inside the mill, the looms were clattering and whirring, but the workers were silent. Hope knew Beaumont was a just employer, there was no denying that. He gave his workers regular breaks and shorter hours than most mill owners. He had also arranged for them to have lessons in the school he'd set up at the mill. He *couldn't* have been responsible for William Kenworthy's death; she prayed it wasn't so.

A man came hurrying over. 'Mr Beaumont, sir, I have been doing all I can to ensure everyone carries on as usual, but it hasn't been easy. The workers are all despondent.'

'Thank you, Robert, it looks as though you have done a splendid job.'

Hope wondered why Beaumont hadn't ordered the mill closed, then she realised that these people relied on every day's work for their livelihood. In spite of her desire to help the poor and uneducated, she still wasn't fully aware of their problems. She sighed and focused on the conversation between the two men. If only she had taken an interest in the mill on her previous visits to Yorkshire, instead of confining herself to the library and school.

'I am here now, and will relieve you

of your supervisory duties. I would like to get some idea of the facts of Mr Kenworthy's death. The coroner may wish to speak to me.'

Robert Latimer lowered his voice. 'I think we should go into the office. There are endless rumours and gossip.'

Inside the main office Beaumont closed the door and gestured to Hope to be seated. 'Now, what were the circumstances of his death?'

Hope's hands shook, and she could see sweat running down Beaumont's temples.

Robert coughed. 'Mr Kenworthy was a fine man, and he was competent and careful. He was found lying at the bottom of the stairs. The doctor who attended him thought there was one likely reason for his accident.'

'What do you mean?' Beaumont asked.

'Alcohol. The doctor thought he'd been drinking. He said he could smell alcohol.'

'No! That's not possible.' Beaumont banged his fist on the desk. 'I imagine this is the rumour circulating. That Mr Kenworthy was a drunk who brought about his own downfall. It isn't true, and I won't have it.'

Hope took his hand. 'Calm down, Beaumont. We'll discover the facts about his death, I'm sure. Don't worry, Robert, my husband isn't angry with you. He's upset.'

'I'm going to find out the truth. Clarence needs to know what happened. Whatever people are saying, anyone who knew him will not believe he was inebriated.' Beaumont dismissed Robert, then said, 'I am sorry, Hope, but I cannot leave the mill yet. I have to meet the workers and reassure them. William was a popular manager. I think it will be better if I do that on my own. How will you occupy yourself? Or would you prefer to return to the house?'

'I shall go to the library if you don't mind, my darling. It's always calming there, and you will know I am close at hand if you need me.'

Beaumont raised his wife's hand to his lips and kissed it. 'I shall always need you, Hope. Always.'

In spite of her sadness at William's death, Hope's heart sang at her husband's words as she let herself out of a side door and skirted the mill on her way to the library at the back of the building. Briefly, she wondered if she should have met with the workers, but she couldn't face that at the moment. Her mind was on the circumstances of William Kenworthy's death.

She shut the door of the library and sank down on a wooden chair. The untidy shelves pleased her as they showed the library was being used. Her idea of allowing books to be borrowed without any records appeared to be working.

She put her head in her hands and took a deep breath. The atmosphere of the room was soothing and her thoughts became clearer.

It was a certainty that she would remain in Yorkshire for a significant period, and she would have to let people know. Mama and Papa would need to be informed, of course, as would the secretary of the suffrage movement. A telephone had been recently installed at the house, so she could get in touch with her parents, but the movement was quite a different matter. She would compose a telegram and have it taken to the post office. That would be one thing off her mind, and then she must concentrate on the business of William Kenworthy. And poor Clarence. As soon as Beaumont was ready to leave the mill, she would suggest they visit him. Unless he had turned up for work at the mill. That would be an awful situation for him to face, with all the horrible rumours circulating.

Hope had just finished writing her message for the telegram, and was browsing among the bookshelves when Beaumont burst into the room. 'Hope, it's no good. I can stand it no more with rumours flying and such ill-feeling. I questioned some of the workers in private, and they seem to confirm the tales about William being drunk. I would swear on my family's life that it is not so!' He sat at the table; Hope noticed the set of his jaw, and knew immediately what he was thinking.

'You wish to visit Clarence, don't you?'

Beaumont's lips lifted in a half-smile. 'You know me well. Yes, I wish to see Clarence. He will be at his father's house. Will you accompany me?'

Hope took his hand, and together they went to look for the young son of Beaumont's friend.

7

They found Clarence sitting on the front step of the house, his head bowed.

'My deepest condolences to you, Clarence; your father was a fine man.' Beaumont sat on the step next to him and put his arm round his shoulder.

Clarence burst into heaving sobs. Hope's heart went out to him, and she wondered how she had ever had doubts about inviting him into their home as part of their family.

'Ophelia and George are very concerned about you,' said Beaumont.

'They came to see me, sir. It was good of them.' Clarence wiped his face with the back of his hand. He took a deep breath. 'Father … Father doesn't … didn't drink.'

'I know. It is a vile rumour.'

The young man lifted his head to look at Beaumont. 'You believe that, even though everyone else thinks he fell because he was drunk?'

'Of course. Your father was a decent man. He liked an occasional whisky or beer, but I have never seen him the worse for drink. It wasn't his nature, even when we were young men. When the others think about it properly they will remember what sort of man he was, and they won't believe he was drunk. Of that I am sure.'

'Thank you, sir, I couldn't have borne it if you'd believed what they were saying. I am angry that people think ill of my father and I can't bear to be anywhere near them.'

'We will get to the bottom of your father's death, but for now we would like you to come and stay with us. We will discuss your future after your father's funeral. What do you think?'

'Yes, please, I'd like that very much. I have been lonely here. The housekeeper has been coming in, but without Father the house is empty.'

'May we help you pack a bag or two?' Hope asked. 'You can easily come back for more things when you need them. I think we should make a start; it will soon be time for luncheon. The twins will be delighted to see you.'

'And I them. Shall we go in?' Clarence led the way into the house, seemingly somewhat lifted from despondency.

Hope deliberately hung back to allow Beaumont and Clarence freedom to talk on the way back to Moorcliff Edge. It was difficult to hear the conversation, and she only caught snippets. Something about investigating, and an intruder. She would question Beaumont later, because she had decided she must solve the mystery of William Kenworthy's death.

★   ★   ★

'Mama, Mama!'

Hope was brought out of her reverie by George's insistent voice. 'Yes, dear, please don't shout.'

Beaumont smiled. 'He had to shout to attract your attention. You were deep in thought. Will you tell us what you were thinking about?'

Hope glanced down the table at Clarence and shook her head. 'Definitely not.'

'The children would like to take a walk on the moor to Rocky Valley, and George wishes to climb the rocks. What do you say?'

'I say, be careful.'

'Thank you, Mama.'

'Thank you … my lady …'

'Please Clarence, you are going to be living here as a member of the family. I will call you Clarence and you must call me Hope. That is my name, after all.'

'Thank you, my — Hope. I would like to go on the moor with Ophelia and George. It will take my mind off my father's death. We often used to walk together. I will remember happy times.'

'That's good. I am sure you have a store of happy memories you can draw on when you're feeling sad.'

'I know Rocky Valley well, it's a good place to go,' Clarence said.

'Don't worry about George, Mama. I will look after him, and I am sure

Clarence will help.' Ophelia smiled at the young man.

George made a face. 'I don't need looking after.'

'Go along, then. You may all get down from the table.'

After the children had left, Hope turned to Beaumont. 'What have you discovered from Clarence about the night William died?'

'He doesn't know much. Just that William went to the mill because he was worried about intruders. There had been signs of damage over the previous few nights. Clarence wanted to go with him, but William wouldn't let him. He said he'd be fine. Clarence says his father had not drunk alcohol that evening because he was planning to do some paperwork.'

'I wonder why someone would want to cause damage at the mill. Have you any idea, Beaumont? Do you think Clarence knows?' Hope was becoming more and more intrigued by this mystery. If only she could get to the bottom of it and clear William's name — not only for

Beaumont, but also for Clarence.

'My dear, you have a certain glow about you. While I should like to think that it is being near me, I believe there is something else that is inflaming you. And I'd also like to know what was occupying your mind a short while ago.'

'Beaumont, of course I enjoy being with you, but I must admit to being interested in poor William's death. It seems such an unlikely circumstance, and I don't like you and Clarence suffering because of it.' Hope was on the verge of admitting to her husband that she would be finding out all she could about the incident, but something told her that it was not a good idea and that Beaumont would make her promise not to interfere. So she changed the subject. 'Clarence is part of the family now. I shall go and see the staff, and particularly ensure Florence and Molly look after him well.'

'Hope, thank you for accepting the boy as you have. I have enough guilt on my shoulders from William's death, and it would only have increased if Clarence had had to live on his own. I shall go to my study and see how I can resolve the question of the house. As you know, it is for the mill manager to live in until his death, and … well, that time has come.'

As Beaumont left the room, Hope suddenly asked, 'Who is William's successor? Who was next in line for the position of manager?'

'I do not wish to be rude, Hope, but that is for me to sort out. You will hear in due course.'

Hope was taken aback by Beaumont's reluctance to tell her. She shrugged her shoulders as Beaumont closed the door firmly behind him.

She went to speak to the servants.

'Certainly, my lady,' said Nanny Swift when Hope explained the situation. 'Of course, he is almost a grown man, and I shall be careful not to treat him as a young child, but I quite understand why he needs nurturing.'

'I knew you would, Florence. You're very intuitive; I've noticed how you treat the twins, and I thank you for it.' Before going to find Molly, she added, 'Please, would you call me Hope, like I asked you?'

'But, my lady, I cannot get used to it at all. It is against protocol.' She let out a long breath. 'Very well, Hope, I shall be honoured.' The two women exchanged smiles.

Now Hope had arranged the household, she sent for Cook and asked her to make sure there were extra-nourishing meals for their guest. As she said the word *guest*, she wanted to amend it to *son*, but that was absurd. She would treat Clarence as if he were her own — but he could never truly be.

★　★　★

Just as Hope was starting to get anxious about the children, she heard their voices and looked out of the drawing room window. There they were, thank goodness. And George was still in one piece. She tried not to be anxious about him, but she was, although she hoped she didn't show it too much. He was getting rather testy lately whenever she or Ophelia were too protective of him. All three were together, rosy-cheeked, although Hope could see that George's breathing was laboured. Clarence was walking slowly by his side as if it was the natural thing to do, and Ophelia had dropped behind.

Hope opened the window to wave at them, but they were engrossed in their conversation. She looked at the three of them and felt her heart fill; three young souls with their lives before them. Ophelia with her hair flowing out behind her, George struggling to keep up with Clarence. And why had she not noticed what a good-looking young man Clarence was? His untidy light brown hair curled around his face, and he was laughing with George, she was pleased to see. She'd already observed his hazel-coloured eyes, and the sadness behind them, but now he looked completely different from the person they'd found sitting desolate on the step of his house. He would be fine, Hope felt sure. Quietly, she closed the window and left the young people to themselves.

★ ★ ★

'Do you truly like it here?' Hope struggled to believe anyone could enjoy living in the north of England, with its dreary buildings and seemingly-constant rain.

'It's a wonderful place. The people in the village and at the mill have made us welcome, and always have a kind word.' Edna handed her friend a cup of tea.

Hope liked sitting in Edna's cosy kitchen. The heat from the range took away the chill she felt after being drenched by a downpour on her walk to the cottage.

Edna continued, 'We can never thank Beaumont enough for offering Thomas a job at the mill. He didn't like his previous job as a delivery man.'

'There was one benefit to his former occupation, Edna. He met you!' The two women laughed. Hope asked, 'Are you happy with your home?'

'It's perfect. We have two bedrooms and the yard at the back.'

Hope was appalled. She hadn't visited Edna and Thomas since their move from London. Two bedrooms with five children was unthinkable.

'You say the people are friendly. Did they like Mr Kenworthy?'

'Oh, yes, he was a fair man. No one had a bad word to say about him as far as I am aware.'

'I don't understand. There are rumours circulating that William Kenworthy fell down the stairs because he was intoxicated.'

'There is no other explanation. The locals are shocked, but what else can they believe? I am very pleased you have taken Clarence into your home.'

'He is a lovely addition to our family, although we won't formally adopt him. He has settled in very well and is a good companion for George.'

'What does Ophelia think about having another boy to contend with?'

'You know Ophelia. She mothers him

116

and he looks at her with puppy-dog eyes. I think he is already a little in love with her. I must confess, it is a joy having another young person around.'

'I sometimes feel guilty, Hope. I have been able to bear children with no difficulties, and you have suffered.'

'I don't begrudge you your children, Edna. I am very happy for you and Thomas. Where are the children now?'

'Playing with their friends. I barely see them except when they are hungry.'

Hope decided she would involve Edna in her investigation. She'd been unsure; but, sitting talking to her friend once again, she realised she would be unable to solve the mystery of William's death without help — and she certainly wouldn't involve Beaumont.

'You will think me foolish, perhaps ...'

Edna giggled. 'I am sorry, Hope, but you have always been quite different from anyone else I have ever known. Imagine, dressing up as a man and visiting a gentlemen's club! Who but you would do that?'

'And you joined me in my adventures! But now I have decided I must discover the truth about William's death. Clarence and Beaumont both insist that he didn't drink to excess. We need to find out more about the intruder, and why William went to the mill that night. Also, if he was unpopular with anyone.'

'What are you saying? It was deliberate? He was killed? No, I can't believe it. Who would do such a thing?'

'That is for us to find out. Will you help me?'

'If you believe there was something suspicious about Mr Kenworthy's death, then of course I will do all in my power to help you.'

'Good, thank you. First, I would like you to talk to Thomas. Find out all you can about how people felt about William ...'

The rest of Hope's visit was taken up with news of Aunt Constance and Hope's parents.

'I'm happy Molly has come to Yorkshire with you. Do tell her I can't wait to see her.'

'I will pass your message on,' Hope assured her. 'You two got on well when you were employed by Aunt Constance. You have both been loyal friends to me.'

'Thomas can't get over the fact that I call you Hope and that we're friends. He thinks I'm being disrespectful, but I told him you're not bothered by convention.'

Hope pulled a face. 'I think I shall have to remain a little aloof at the mill. I know no one there, and I think I must behave decorously.' A cold shiver ran down Hope's spine as she said the words, knowing she would be where William Kenworthy had been killed. Her hands shook as a word formed in her mind: she would be investigating a *murder*.

★   ★   ★

Beaumont sat in his office at Moorcliff Edge, staring out of the window. He should be attending to the papers in front of him, but he couldn't concentrate on anything except the death of his dear friend. He raised a hand to his quivering lips and clenched his jaw, swallowing hard.

How could he think about a successor to William? There was no one who could hold a candle to his old friend and his administration of the mill. Beaumont owed everything to him. Then he thought of Clarence, and how dear Hope had accepted him so readily after only a moment's hesitation. She had always been a large-hearted woman, and he loved her dearly. He'd been disappointed at their lack of closeness recently, but Hope seemed to have a lightness about her now — which was surprising, as he knew she hated Yorkshire. It was good of her to be as receptive to the move as she had been. He was sure the children, especially George, would benefit from their stay here. He would like it to be a permanent transfer, but wouldn't inflict something on Hope if she was set against it.

A knock at the door startled him. He blinked rapidly and said a gruff, 'Come in.' He looked up as a man entered.

'Mr Beaumont, sir, I have come to offer

my condolences to you. Mr Kenworthy will be missed; he was an admirable manager.'

'Sidney, thank you. I am grateful for your words.'

Sidney Potter turned to leave. Then he looked back and said, 'Will we have a new manager soon? At the moment, no one is sure who is in charge. Obviously you are, sir, but on the factory floor there is no one running things except Robert Latimer, and he's struggling.'

'Of course. I am here to sort out many things, Sidney, and one of them is the new manager.'

Sidney cleared his throat and said, 'I wonder if I might be considered for the position, sir? I do have experience as I stood in for William Kenworthy when he had other business to attend to. Also, I have been at the mill for a long time, and I know how it should operate.'

'I'll bear that in mind,' replied Beaumont, surprised at the self-assurance of his employee.

After he had left, Beaumont reflected

that perhaps it wasn't presumptuousness, just astuteness, which motivated Sidney to put himself forward. He could be a man worth considering. Knowing that he should make a priority of appointing a new mill manager, he sifted through the paperwork on his desk and drew up a small list of possible names.

After an hour of scrutinising the papers in front of him, Beaumont decided to face the task of arranging William's funeral — with the approval of Clarence, of course.

Another knock at the door made him sigh, and he was particularly surprised when Nanny Swift entered the room, as Hope generally dealt with household and staffing matters.

'I'm sorry to bother you, Mr Beaumont, but I wasn't sure who else to speak to about the matter. I am unable to find Lady Hope to tell her.'

Seeing the worry etched on her face, Beaumont wanted to reassure her. 'I will help if I am able.'

'It's just that I saw a strange man

leaving the house. He looked shifty, as though he didn't want anyone to see him.'

'Sidney Potter has recently visited me. He works at the mill. He has a moustache, wears spectacles, and was smartly dressed. Was that the man?'

'No, it wasn't. This man was wearing labourer's clothes and was clean-shaven. And he left by the back entrance, past the scullery. He was a handsome chap with fine skin. He scurried out of the house.'

'I see.' His wife was up to her old tricks. He chuckled. Why was she going out dressed as a man? 'I know that man. You have no need to worry. Please see to your duties — but if you are ever concerned about anything at all, don't hesitate to ask me.'

'Thank you, Mr Beaumont,' she said and left the room.

Beaumont puzzled for a while as to why Hope was impersonating a man again. He wouldn't enquire; in time, he was sure he would either find out or be told the answer.

* * *

'Edna, you make a very fine man. Are they Thomas's clothes you are wearing?'

'They are. It wasn't a problem sorting out some clothes to wear. My problem was leaving Thomas with the children to deal with. I rarely go out in the evening. How did you get away?'

'I left much earlier. I have been walking on the moor and thinking. I was surprised how pleasant it was. I enjoyed the tranquillity obtained from being totally alone in that vast sublime landscape. *And* it didn't rain!'

'It doesn't rain here as much as you southerners think.'

'But you are a souther —' Hope caught Edna's eye and they laughed together.

'So what did Beaumont say when you said you were going out?'

'I didn't tell him. I told Molly to leave it a while, then tell him I had gone visiting. I am still not sure why you think we need to go to a public house to further our investigation.'

'Thomas says everything is discussed there, from Mrs Young's bunions to what the Kaiser is doing. I think we may discover something of importance. If not, we will have had some fun.'

'No one must recognise me, Edna.'

'I can assure you, they won't. Not in those clothes. Wherever did you find them?'

'The gardener had left some things in a shed. It's a good thing he's left Moorcliff Edge, or he might accuse me of stealing. Although they're not very nice, are they?' Hope looked down at the frayed jacket and coarse trousers with a patch on one knee.

'They're exactly right. We'll blend in with the other men at the pub. I'm looking forward to our evening, Hope, but it's nice to have some time here by the river. It's really calming. I never seem to have a moment to myself.'

'I think the twins and Clarence would enjoy coming here,' said Hope, imagining them sitting on the bridge as she and Edna were. In the summer, they could swim in the clear water, and perhaps catch some fish ... What was she thinking? In her mind, she had already accepted the fact they would all still be in Yorkshire well into the following year. Perhaps it would be no bad thing. This was Clarence's home and she shouldn't think of uprooting him until he was ready, and the twins had not objected to the move. 'We can stay a little longer, Edna. You must enjoy some free time. Then we shall go and eavesdrop.'

After some more reminiscences, Hope and Edna walked back to the village and entered the public house. Hope's heart was in her mouth and her pulse quickened. It would be unseemly for the wife of the mill owner to be found in the compromising position of being not only dressed as a man, but also drinking intoxicating liquor in a hostelry.

Edna swaggered to the bar. 'Two glasses of your best ale.'

Hope had to look away or she knew she'd explode with laughter. The place was crowded, but she located some seats in the middle of the room. That would be a good position to observe what was going on.

Edna carried the beer to the table, sloshing some of it across the scratched wood. Hope took a sip and tried not to shudder at the bitter taste.

They pretended to be engrossed in conversation, but they both surreptitiously looked around and listened to what was being said.

'Poor Kenworthy, what a way to end up. You'd have thought he could remain sober for the sake of his son, wouldn't you?'

Someone else put in, 'I must say, I've never seen him the worse for drink, *never*, and I've lived around here all my life. He didn't ever come in here, did he?'

'Drinking alone at home. That's bad. Mind you, he lost his wife. That could drive a man to drink.'

'Surely someone would have known he had a problem and we'd have heard about it. You can't keep secrets here. It's very strange,' added another.

'There's no other explanation as far

as I can see. Just goes to show, you never really know people. The fine, upstanding Mr Kenworthy, killed by his taste for the demon drink.'

A man entered and, without greeting anyone, ordered his drink. He was tall, with dark brown hair and a moustache, plus a pair of spectacles perched on his nose. His clothes were stylish, but Hope didn't recognise him.

The stranger finished his drink quickly, and left the establishment soon after. Edna nudged Hope and signalled for them to follow him.

'Who is he?' whispered Hope, once they were outside, with a distance between them and the man.

'He's Sidney Potter. He does the accounts at the mill. My Thomas doesn't like him. Let's see what he's up to.'

Thinking he was probably merely going home for the night, Hope trailed after Edna, who suddenly pulled her into a dark alley. 'What's ...' Then Hope felt Edna's finger on her lips and held her breath.

'Are you following me?' snarled Sidney Potter.

Hope widened her eyes and trembled. She saw another person emerge from the shadows, and relaxed slightly, listening intently.

'I need the money you owe me,' stated the man.

'You'll get it when I'm good and ready. I told you not to come anywhere near me.' Sidney Potter started to stride off, but the other man held onto his jacket.

'I need the money! If I didn't need it desperately for my sick wife, I would never have agreed to lure Mr Kenworthy to the mill the night he died!'

Potter reached into his pocket, took out a wad of notes, and flung them on the ground in front of the man. 'Take it! And if I ever hear or even see you again, I'll be sending for the authorities. Who do you think they'll believe? The new manager at Beaumont's mill, or a snivelling tyke like you?'

The men's footsteps could be heard retreating in opposite directions, and Hope let out the breath she had been holding. 'How dare he refer to my husband as 'Beaumont'?' she whispered, indignantly.

'I was more intent on working out who the other man was,' said Edna.

'Of course; I was being selfish. Have you any inkling as to who he could be?'

Edna shook her head. 'I am good at distinguishing voices. I'll visit the mill tomorrow with some excuse, and see if I can find out.'

★ ★ ★

'Ah, Hope, I wondered where you were. Molly simply told me you were out visiting. At this time!' Beaumont wondered what excuse she would give for her absence. He had heard Hope running up the stairs, and her arrival in the drawing room looking somewhat dishevelled confirmed that she had been upstairs to change into her usual clothes.

'I have been with Edna. It was wonderful to see her. You will have to get used to me disappearing, and us spending time together. It is one of the advantages of being here.'

'There are others?' he teased.

'Maybe.'

He patted the seat of the sofa. 'Come and sit close to me. We spend too little time together. William's death has taught me that we must make the most of every moment of our lives, as we can never be sure what awaits us.' After Hope had settled herself next to him, he cuddled her. 'How do you think Clarence is bearing up?'

'Well, I think. Our children are helping him greatly, I am sure. Ophelia told me they have been in the gardens with him, and he has been telling them how he would change things.'

'Clearing the weeds would be the first thing to do. Since the head gardener left, the place hasn't been properly managed. But, more importantly, is it right for me to discourage Clarence from returning to the mill to work until after the funeral?'

'I think it is best to leave Clarence to decide for himself. At present, he seems to want to be away from the mill — and who can blame him?'

'Indeed. I feel it myself. I prefer to work here in the study rather than at the office, although I know I must go as there is no one to supervise the mill now.' Beaumont was enjoying the newfound closeness between him and his wife. It was almost like when they were first married. 'I have been drawing up a list of possible managers. It was strange today … I had a visit from Sidney Potter. I have probably spoken to you about him: he is a bookkeeper. It surprised and pleased me that he came to the house to offer his condolences.' Beaumont felt Hope's body stiffen. 'What is it, darling?'

'Nothing. I am tired, that is all. Did this Sidney have anything else to say?'

'I was somewhat surprised when he suggested himself as a suitable candidate for the position of mill manager.'

'Did he? And is he a suitable candidate in your eyes?'

Beaumont was startled by her question. 'He has been employed by me for many years, and is hard-working, efficient, and honest.'

'Do the workers like him as they did William?'

'Of that, I am not so sure. He is not a particularly sociable fellow.'

'And what about you, Beaumont? Do you respect him?'

'I am beginning to feel as though I am on the witness stand! I don't feel strongly about him, but he is on my list, and I will interview him for the post. Let us change the subject. No, I have a better idea ...'Then he kissed her with intensity, delighted at her response to his passion.

8

It was the day of William Kenworthy's funeral. Beaumont had given the mill workers the day off with a promise that they would be paid in full.

Clarence was dressed in a new suit, which Beaumont had taken him to be fitted for, and Ophelia and George were fussing around him. 'We'll be beside you,' said Ophelia, taking his arm and smiling up at him.

Hope thought poor Clarence was torn between grief for his father, and the feeling that he needed to appear strong. 'You look splendid, Clarence, a credit to your father,' said Hope. 'Are we ready?' She looked to her husband for guidance. Her experience of funerals was small, she was pleased to admit.

'The cortège will be starting from William's house, so we will walk the short distance, if you're all in agreement. What about you, George, can you manage?'

'Yes, Father, I know I can.'

Hope was amazed. That was the first time she'd heard her son refer to Beaumont as 'Father' — it was usually 'Papa'. Then she realised he was emulating Clarence, who had become something of a hero to him with his knowledge of the moors and his capability in doing various jobs on the estate.

They arrived at the house and stood outside as Beaumont directed the casket to be placed on the hearse. The horses that would be pulling the black-lacquered carriage looked magnificent in the early autumn sun: they remained perfectly still as if sensing the significance of the day. Then the procession to the church began.

Clarence and Beaumont, with Hope and the twins close behind them, led the mourners to the churchyard. Villagers stopped and bowed their heads as the carriage passed by.

Hope knew it wasn't seemly for women to attend funerals — although the rules had loosened a little since Queen

Victoria's death — but she felt she had to be present, and had no qualms about Ophelia also being there. She didn't want to cause offence, so she would remain in the background.

At the church, Clarence took his place at the head of his father's coffin, and Beaumont stood at the foot. He gave the young man a reassuring nod, Hope noted from her pew seat. Beside her, she heard George's laboured breathing, but didn't fuss over him; he'd done remarkably well with the walk to the house, and then on to the church. There would be time now for him to sit still and recover. Hope relaxed a little, and thought how her family was changing: her life was taking a new direction and, despite these tragic circumstances, she was looking forward to the future.

Many voices swelled the hymns; it was gratifying to know that there was a large congregation. As she bent her head in prayer, she inhaled the sweet fragrance of the dark crimson roses and freesias. She knew Clarence had chosen them especially because they symbolised sorrow, respect, and trust.

Following the service, Beaumont walked with Clarence to the grave. Hope felt goosebumps, and wanted to gather her children close to her, but she resisted. They were coping well. She could see Beaumont, Clarence, and the vicar in conversation, and wondered what was happening.

Then Beaumont stepped forward, faced the mourners and said: 'I stand here, torn between wretchedness and pride. Wretchedness because my dear friend is dead, and I will no longer be able to enjoy his remarkable company or hear his voice again. And pride, because his son Clarence epitomises everything William stood for: self-respect, respect for others, hard work, and honesty.'

Hope trembled at her husband's words. Tears trickled down her cheeks, and George's hand crept into hers and give it a squeeze.

Clarence threw earth on top of the casket as the vicar intoned, 'Earth to earth, ashes to ashes, dust to dust ...'

The mourners made their way home, and Hope glimpsed Edna, standing apart by some trees. Now was not the time to do more than raise her hand in acknowledgement. She would see her later, as Nanny Swift had been asked to look after Edna's young children.

Normally there would have been a funeral meal, which Beaumont had offered to host at Moorcliff Edge, but Clarence had been adamant that he wanted nothing of the sort. Until his father's name was cleared, he didn't feel able to have anything to do with his fellow workers at the mill. So the five of them trudged home.

The atmosphere lightened a little after they had all changed their clothes and had a reviving cup of tea. Ophelia and George took the praxinoscope to the sitting room to show Clarence, who was as delighted with it as they were. 'I could make one of those,' he declared. 'Or at least, I could try.'

'I'm sure you could do anything you

want to, Clarence,' declared Ophelia.

'I know what I *don't* want to do,' burst out Clarence. 'I don't want to go back to work at the mill — but I'll have to, won't I? Should I go tomorrow, or perhaps the day after?' His face clouded.

'Clarence,' said Beaumont, putting his hand on the boy's shoulder, 'I realise how difficult it could be for you to return to the mill. You do not have to yet. Why not take some time to grieve for your father and adjust to your new surroundings? Perhaps you could defer going back until the new year — what do you think?'

'Thank you; I would be pleased not to have to go back just yet. I would like to do some work in the gardens — the vegetable plot needs clearing, and there are walls to repair around the estate. Would you like to learn how to repair a dry stone wall, George?'

George nodded, and Ophelia said, 'Is there no end to your talents?'

When the children had left the room, Hope wasn't sure what to say to her husband. The silence was broken by

139

Beaumont.

'You have been a great support to me, Hope. It has been a difficult time, and I doubt I would have managed without you by my side. I feel as though we have overcome an obstacle today, and I will now be able to progress at the mill. As you know, last week I interviewed several men for the position of mill manager, and I have made my choice. I am going to appoint Sidney Potter. He has been particularly helpful recently, and I think he is a good, honest man.'

Hope was speechless. She wanted to warn Beaumont against the man — but how could she, when she had no concrete evidence to prove he wasn't the upright person Beaumont thought? She had only overheard a conversation between Sidney Potter and a man she couldn't name. She remembered that Edna would be arriving at the house soon, so excused herself and went to wait for her friend. Nanny Swift had some games planned for the children, and Ophelia had promised to help entertain them.

★   ★   ★

As they walked around the grounds, the two women discussed the funeral which had been overshadowed by the circumstances surrounding William's death.

'It was a good turnout. I hope Clarence can start to get on with his life again now. He isn't keen to go back to the mill. That is the main reason I want us to solve how William really died — so that his son can proudly face the other workers. Did you find out who the other man was, Edna?'

'I didn't hear his voice at the mill — there are too many people working there for me to talk to everyone — but I have found out which of the workers have a sick wife. There are several. I am going to make a point of encountering them in the next few days.'

'Good. Would it help if I sent you to them with food parcels? It would give you a legitimate reason to call.'

'An excellent idea.'

'The funeral made me think about

141

mortality. We simply never know at what point our lives will be taken from us. I am pleased now that I agreed to come to Yorkshire, and that we have taken Clarence into our home … and hearts. Beaumont and I are close again. You can't imagine how happy that makes me. If I were to die tomorrow, I should have no regrets.'

'Don't say such things, Hope! It scares me, especially when we are investigating some very suspicious circumstances. If it weren't for Clarence, I would suggest we shouldn't meddle.'

The early evening turned chilly, and the women returned to the warmth of the house. It was good to hear laughter coming from the nursery. Nanny Swift was indeed an asset to the family. She'd been most interested to hear that Hope had met Edna while she was a maid at her aunt's London residence. And she hadn't appeared shocked that the two of them had become friends.

Edna collected her children, who were reluctant to leave Moorcliff Edge. Ophelia assured them they would be able to visit again soon.

When they'd left, the twins packed away the toys and games, and Clarence followed Hope out of the room. 'Was it all right for me to relax with the children, Hope? I don't want anyone to think I was being disrespectful to my father, especially on the day of his funeral.'

'Oh, Clarence, I am sure your father would be pleased to know that you are carrying on with your life. He was a pillar of support to you during your formative years, and I have no doubt you will be the man he wanted you to be. Beaumont esteemed your father, as you know, and he doesn't do that lightly.' As she said the words, Hope knew she was wrong: Beaumont held Sidney Potter in high regard, and he deserved nothing but his comeuppance!

★　★　★

Over the following days, Clarence fell into a routine of getting up early, breakfasting, and then taking himself into the garden. This morning, Hope wrapped a shawl around her shoulders and went to find him, with the excuse of offering him a cup of tea. 'There you are, Clarence, working hard as usual. What are you doing today?'

'I thought it would be a good idea to fix up a feeder for the birds. Yesterday, while it was raining, I sat in the shed and made one. What do you think?' He held up an intricate construction which resembled a little open-sided house with a sloped wooden roof.

Hope clapped her hands with glee. 'It's beautiful! What a lovely idea, Clarence. Could you make some more, and dot them all around the grounds? It will enhance my walks to be able to view the birds feeding.'

'I can do that. Except around the vegetable garden, of course.' He smiled his sweet smile, and it was all Hope could do not to clasp him to her. What a delight he was! 'I think George might be interested in helping me, if that's all right with you.'

Deciding not to voice her concern that the cold, damp air might be bad for her son's chest, she merely nodded her head

144

and said, 'Of course, if he's in agreement.' She watched as Clarence attached the feeder to a stout branch of an apple tree. 'May I ask you something else? You do not have to answer if it distresses you, but I wondered what happened the night of your dear father's death. What caused him to go to the mill?' Hope held her breath, not wanting to upset Clarence, but desperately needing an answer.

He shrugged his shoulders and said, 'Father had a caller late that evening, and then he told me he had to go to the mill as he wanted to investigate the damage caused by the intruder. It was easier while the place was empty. I told Beaumont about it.'

'Were you worried about him being there alone?' probed Hope.

'Not really.'

Hope's heart missed a beat. 'Did you tell Beaumont about the caller to your house?'

'I can't remember. Is it important?' Clarence appeared to have lost interest in the conversation and was looking towards the shed.

'You carry on with your work. I shall get Cook to look out some food for the birds as well as the mill workers,' she laughed as she made her way back to the house, completely forgetting about the tea she was supposed to be offering Clarence.

Hope couldn't wait to see Edna, but she had to. Today, Edna was taking some food parcels to the mill workers and she would call at Moorcliff Edge on her return. Busying herself with household matters, the time passed slowly. At last Edna arrived, breathless and pink.

'I think I've found him,' she burst out without preamble. 'He used to work at the mill, but had to stay at home to look after his wife and their young children.'

'But how does he live without an income?' Hope was horrified at the situation. If one family was existing like that, how many others were there? She had been campaigning for women's right to vote — perhaps she should have been concentrating on the rights of sick people and their families. But for now, she concerned herself with finding out more from Edna.

'I can take you to him if you like. I didn't tackle him on the issue of Mr Kenworthy, as I didn't want to make him suspicious.' Edna flopped down in a chair. 'I've been scurrying round with food for so many people. We really are lucky with our situations, aren't we, Hope?'

Hope compared her circumstances with Edna's, and reluctantly agreed. 'We'll go to see him again tomorrow and take another parcel, shall we? Or would you prefer me to go on my own?'

'I think it best if you go, Hope, if you don't mind. I have things to catch up on which I let slide today, and then there are the children.'

Hope formed a plan in her mind as she ordered tea for the two of them.

★　★　★

The next day, Hope asked the children how they were going to spend their time. Ophelia took her mother to one side and said, 'George is doing too much, I feel. I shall suggest to him that we create some images for the praxinoscope.'

'How thoughtful you are, darling.' She dropped a kiss on her daughter's head and smoothed down her hair.

'Clarence, what will you do? Will you join the twins in their activities?'

He cleared his throat and looked down. 'I was hoping to talk to Beaumont, but I think he's already left for the mill.'

Hope nodded. 'Is there anything I can help you with?' She hoped the boy wasn't troubled; he'd been remarkably strong about his father's death.

'It's just that Beaumont said that, as I was to live here, the house Father and I shared will be allocated to the new manager. I know that's the way of things, but there are still many of our possessions there, and ...'

'Of course,' said Hope. 'We must help you move them here, to your new home. Shall I help you start on them?'

'Father's clothes are no good to me, and I'm sure no one from the mill would appreciate them, not when they seem to be so against him. They are quite wrong. Father didn't drink.' He paused. 'What am I to do with them?'

Suddenly, Hope knew exactly what. 'Let's go to your old home now.'

Together, they packed many of William Kenworthy's belongings, and left them in the hall of the house for collection by the chauffeur from Moorcliff Edge. Hope picked up a particularly fine jacket and coat and said, 'I know someone who could benefit from a warm winter garment. Would you come with me to give it to him?'

* * *

Tobias Smith opened the door cautiously, and frowned when he saw Hope and Clarence. 'Can I help you?' he asked, glancing back inside the house.

'I am Lady Hope Beaumont. My husband owns the mill. It has come to our notice that you may be living in straitened circumstances, and we would like to offer help.'

149

'Someone called with a food parcel yesterday and we are grateful.' Tobias kept looking at Clarence.

'The autumn days are getting chillier, and we have a coat and jacket which may be of use to you,' said Hope, indicating to Clarence that he should hand it over. 'I have heard your wife is unwell. Is there anything we can do to aid her?'

'The doctor will call later today.'

'May I come in and see her?' asked Hope, wanting to give Tobias no alternative but to admit her.

'She's resting,' was all he said. 'Thank you for calling.' And he shut the door.

Clarence clutched at Hope's arm in agitation. 'Sorry, my — Hope. That was the man who came to the house and accompanied Father to the mill on the night he met his death. Shall I knock on the door again and ask him about it?'

'No,' replied Hope. 'I will tell Beaumont tonight when he returns home, and see what he has to say.'

On the short journey back to Moorcliff Edge, Hope could hardly contain the tension that mounted inside her. If Tobias could confirm it was Sidney Potter who had sent him to William's house and told him to go to the mill, then it was possible that William Kenworthy's reputation would be restored, and Clarence would gain peace.

★   ★   ★

Hope had itched to go to the mill and speak to Beaumont immediately, and dinner seemed interminable. When the children had gone to bed, she sat in the drawing room with her husband.

'Was your day a good one?' she asked.

He nodded. 'And yours? What have you been doing?'

'Clarence and I cleared out William's clothes, and we took some to a man called Tobias Smith.'

'Good.'

'But it isn't good in any way, Beaumont. He was one of your workers, and has left his job to care for his sick wife and children. How is that good? He has no income.'

'I see. What do they live on?'

'Charity, I imagine, and Tobias has taken money from someone to do something underhand. I am not sure I quite understand events myself.'

'You are quite overwrought, Hope. Please share your burden. Maybe I can help.'

Hope stopped pacing back and forth in front of the fireplace and sat next to her husband. 'Tobias Smith went to the Kenworthys' house on the night of William's death, and enticed him to the mill on the pretext that there was damage.'

'I already knew why William went to the mill. Over the past few weeks, damage to the machinery had been found on several mornings. It is quite likely that there had been damage that evening.'

'How would Tobias know? He wouldn't have been in the mill after it had closed. Edna and I know the truth of the matter.'

Beaumont appeared to be listening intently as Hope explained how they'd overheard Sidney and Tobias talking.

'You are saying that Sidney paid Tobias to lure William to the mill? Why?'

'I am not sure.' Hope still had no proof that Sidney had been instrumental in William's death. 'You must speak to Tobias and see if he knows anything more. He was reluctant to talk to me.'

Beaumont leapt up. 'I will go now.' He clenched his fists. 'I will find out who is responsible for William's death, and that person will get the punishment he deserves.'

'Please, calm down. You cannot go now. His children will be asleep and raised voices will wake them. I don't believe Tobias played any part in William's death beyond luring him to the mill. I have no proof, so will not make accusations against anyone else yet. You must visit Tobias first thing in the morning, and see if he can tell you anything more about the whole matter. I have the feeling he is hiding something.'

'Very well, I will take your advice — although I am quite sure I shall get no rest tonight.'

153

As Beaumont walked to the dwelling that Hope had described, he tried to quell his anger. He must remain calm and get to the truth. If, however, Tobias was responsible for William's death, Beaumont knew he'd find it difficult to control his wrath.

He banged on the cottage door and entered the kitchen without waiting for an answer. Immediately, all his anger drained away. A youngish man who looked tired and dishevelled was feeding porridge to a small baby, while three other children sat round the table, wide-eyed at the sight of the stranger, each clutching a small piece of dry bread.

Tobias appeared alarmed. 'Mr Beaumont!' He began to brush away crumbs and wipe at the table with a cloth.

Beaumont touched his arm. 'Tobias, I am not here to cause you unease, but we must talk. Perhaps I should come back later. You all seem occupied at the moment.' He tried to give a reassuring

154

smile, but his mouth would not respond. These poor people. If he had to hand over Tobias to the authorities, how would the children survive? Or his sick wife?

'I understand, sir. Perhaps we could go outside.' Tobias took a thick coat from the back of the door and huddled himself into it as the two men left the house.

Once outside, Tobias said, 'I think I know why you're here. It cannot be a coincidence that we receive a food parcel, some warm clothes, and a visit from you without good cause. Except in this case, it's a bad cause, very bad indeed.' Tobias shook his head and shivered.

Beaumont was unsure how to continue. 'Whatever the outcome of our conversation, Tobias, I give you my word that your family will be provided for. All I seek is the truth. Do you know how Mr Kenworthy met his death?'

Tobias seemed to shrivel before Beaumont's eyes and his face went pale. Eventually, he nodded. 'Yes, I do.' He gave a chesty cough and wiped at his eyes with a piece of dirty rag. 'I don't want to carry the burden of this any longer. I was told to call on Mr Kenworthy and tell him to come to the mill with me. You must have known about the broken machinery and suchlike.' Beaumont nodded. 'We went up to the second floor, and then things happened so quickly. Mr Kenworthy was hurled down the stairs, and I was told to throw some whisky over him — to make it smell as if he'd been drinking, I suppose. Then I had to place a flask in his pocket. By that time, I knew he was dead.' Tobias closed his eyes and shuddered. 'I was an unwilling accomplice, Mr Beaumont, but I had my family to provide for, and I was offered a considerable sum of money.'

'By whom?' Beaumont needed confirmation.

'Sidney Potter.'

Then Tobias returned to the house and slammed the door shut.

Beaumont raged as he strode from Tobias's house to the mill, but tried to calm himself when he entered the building. Already the workers were at their duties, and he saw Sidney Potter in the office with Robert.

Potter looked up from his papers and took off his spectacles. 'Is there anything I can do to help you, Mr Beaumont?'

'There is,' he said. 'No, Robert, please don't go, I should like you to remain and hear what I have to say.' Beaumont was pleased to have a witness. 'Sidney, I have it on good authority that you are the person responsible for William Kenworthy's death. What have you to say for yourself?'

Potter frowned, and then started to laugh. 'Who told you that? Some worker who has it in for me, I'll be bound.'

'Something like that,' replied Beaumont. 'If I said it was a certain Mr Smith, how would you respond?'

'Tobias Smith has lost his mind,' spluttered Sidney Potter. 'You can safely disregard anything he tells you.'

'As far as I am aware, there are at least seven Smiths in this mill alone — so why do you fix on this man, Tobias, who does not even work here now? You could have chosen any one of them.' Beaumont was now sure of Potter's guilt, but the fight had gone out of him; he felt grief at his friend's murder rather than anger at his killer.

'Robert, tell Beaumont about Tobias Smith, how he would lie about anything. The man has no moral scruples,' said Sidney Potter.

But Robert shook his head and backed away. 'Tobias is a good man. I would believe anything he told me.'

'Rather than what *I* tell you?'

'Yes, definitely,' replied Robert.

He moved to stand next to Beaumont, who said, 'We shall send for the authorities; and may God help you, Potter.'

★　★　★

'What will become of Tobias Smith? And his family?' Hope had mixed feelings about her part in the affair. Clarence would once again be able to hold his head up high in the village, Sidney Potter would be tried for murder, but what of Tobias Smith?

'I understand his motive for doing Potter's bidding, as I too would do anything for you and the children. I will do everything in my power to keep Tobias Smith at home with his family, but I have realised I must ensure that the mill workers, past and present, are never in circumstances where they have to resort to dishonesty.'

'That is a huge undertaking.'

'And one I can only contemplate, knowing I have your support.'

Hope joined Beaumont at the drawing room window and looked out. Clarence was once again working in the garden. He was busy cutting dead wood from the plants in the herbaceous border.

'Will you tell Clarence?' Hope asked.

'I shall. And before he hears it from another source. He is growing into a fine young man. I think he will take the news well. He will be angry, of course, but relieved that his father was in no way at fault. Poor William! To lose his life at such an age, and in such a way. It is almost more than I can bear.'

In silence, they clung to each other,

159

and Hope wondered why she had been loath to come to Moorcliff Edge. She belonged by his side.

When Beaumont had calmed down, he left the room, and Hope watched as he joined Clarence outside. Together, they walked away from the house, Beaumont's arm protectively around the young man's shoulders.

As she wondered whether to join the children for luncheon, it occurred to her that there was no motive for Potter to kill William. Why had Beaumont not thought of that? Or had he? Without a clear motive, there would be less chance of a conviction. There was only one person to discuss this with.

★   ★   ★

'Don't be shy, Hope; take as much as you like, we have plenty.'

Hope liked sitting at Edna's kitchen table. The atmosphere was relaxed and noisy. In spite of her worries, she felt hungry, and did as Edna told her. They could talk after the meal.

'Children, when you have finished your bread and cheese, take your apples outside to eat. We wish to talk.'

Edna poured tea and passed a cup to Hope. 'I have heard rumours as to what's happened. People are saying Sidney Potter and Tobias Smith have been taken away by the authorities to be questioned in connection with Mr Kenworthy's death. Is that right?'

'It is. And thanks to you, Potter will receive the justice he deserves,' Hope said.

'You did not say that with confidence. There is something bothering you.'

'You know me better than I know myself. There is no motive. What motive did Potter have?'

'He would become mill manager once Mr Kenworthy was out of the way. Was that what he wanted?'

'I don't think so. That was just a happy unanticipated extra for him. There has to be something else.'

Edna sat quietly for a moment. 'I told you my Thomas didn't like him. He said he heard Sidney and Mr Kenworthy arguing heatedly not long ago. They were in the office and Mr Kenworthy was shaking a book in his face.'

'A book? What type of book?'

'I didn't ask. Is it important?'

'I believe it may be. I am going to the mill office to see what I can discover.' Hope was sorry to cut her visit to Edna's house short, but it was necessary to examine the contents of the office before anyone else did.

She passed by the mill's busy workers, who glanced at her curiously. Once inside Sidney Potter's office, she closed the door and sat at the desk. There were several large books lined up, and she pulled one towards her and opened it. Long columns of figures confused her and referred to things she didn't understand, but after a while she recognised a pattern, and cross-referenced the items as best she could. There were regular entries for supplies — and other records which involved quite large sums of money going out to the same name each month. Hope grabbed a piece of paper, wrote down the amounts and the payee, replaced the books and left the room.

As she made her way home, she tried to figure out what it could all mean. Sidney Potter was guilty of murder, of that she was sure. But why would he risk being hanged? Money, it had to be money that was the motive. And she felt sure the piece of paper in the pocket of her skirt held the key.

9

Beaumont explained everything to Hope. They were both flabbergasted by Sidney Potter's mendacity.

'We should have guessed the motive, Hope. It was purely and simply money. Sidney Potter, my bookkeeper, had been embezzling funds from the mill for a long time, it would appear. He had several bank accounts in different names, and siphoned off regular payments into them.'

'And William found out and challenged him,' said Hope. 'Did he say anything to you about it? Shouldn't he have told you first?'

'If only he had,' sighed Beaumont, 'I might have been able to step in and prevent his murder. I imagine he wanted to solve the problem without troubling me.'

'But why did Sidney want to be mill manager? Wouldn't it have taken away his responsibility for the accounting?' Hope wondered.

'He wanted to do both jobs.' Beaumont gave a mirthless laugh. 'He said he would be pleased to help out.'

'Beaumont,' said Hope, 'you must try and put this from your mind; we all must. Poor William is dead, and we mourn him, but we must think of the future. Clarence is dealing bravely with his loss, George's health is much improved, and Ophelia — well, she adores having you around more.'

Beaumont put his arms around his wife. 'Hope, you are a wonderful woman and I love you dearly. Have you any regrets about being in Yorkshire? I expect you miss your suffragette meetings, don't you? And your circle of friends.'

Hope snuggled into him. 'It's nice being with you, and it's wonderful to have Edna so near. No doubt the suffragettes will continue without me, but I do still support them in my heart.'

'I do, too,' said Beaumont.

Hope pushed herself away from him and stared at him. 'You? You couldn't care less about them.'

'That's not true. I agree with much of what they are campaigning for. What I was against was the fact that the meetings and rallies tired you out as much as they did, that's all. If I were a member of parliament, I would definitely support women's suffrage. Women, just as much as men, are sensible enough to vote.'

Hope collapsed against him. 'I wish you'd explained all of this to me before. I thought you were a hard-hearted beast and I very nearly hated you.'

'You must never do that,' exclaimed Beaumont.

'Why not?' asked Hope, indignant that she'd misunderstood her husband for so long.

'Because we belong together, you and I. We are two halves of a whole and always will be. I love you, Hope Beaumont.'

★   ★   ★

'Aha, found you at last!' Beaumont came up behind Hope and grasped her waist.

166

She held a spray of mistletoe above their heads, and turned to kiss him.

When they drew apart, he said, 'I feel somewhat redundant at the mill. Robert is proving to be an excellent manager and everything is running smoothly. I have been thinking that we should return to London for Christmas and remain there. I will once again make short visits back here. I know you didn't want to live in Yorkshire, and Clarence can decide whether to come with us or remain here.' Beaumont fiddled with a piece of ivy while Hope cut some sprigs of holly.

'You might have told me your plans before I started on the Christmas wreaths,' Hope teased.

'We will take them with us.'

'No, we won't!'

Beaumont looked startled.

'We are staying here. We are all happy, even me. I have everything I could wish for. It is hard to admit it, but you were right about George's health. He is much better and leading a more active life than I could ever have imagined. He and

167

Clarence cut all this greenery this morning, and now they have gone walking on the moor with Ophelia. I have been thinking how sad it will be for them all when Clarence goes back to work at the mill in the new year. Please hold this while I wrap the ivy round.'

'Like this?'

Hope nodded.

Beaumont said, 'I am amazed that you would choose to remain here. As for Clarence, I believe he has found his vocation. He appears at his happiest when working in the garden. If we are to stay here, then, as we no longer have a head gardener, why don't I offer the job to Clarence?'

'That's a wonderful idea. It will be his best Christmas present, I am sure.'

'I have been thinking about presents. Your mama and papa mentioned a big journey in the spring, and I remember your desire to travel more after we visited Paris. I requested some information which arrived this morning. If you would like to go adventuring with your parents, then that shall be your Christmas gift.'

Hope fingered the necklace she was wearing. 'You give marvellous presents. I may no longer be involved with the suffragettes, but I support them in my heart. See, I am wearing the suffragette necklace you gave me. As for going away, how could I leave you all?'

'The children will go with you. All three of them, if they would like to. Ophelia and George would benefit from time with their grandparents. I would come too, but I have some major contracts to oversee, so need to remain in the country.'

'I don't want to leave you, Beaumont; not now, not ever.'

'It's a holiday, Hope. You would return, and everything will be as it is now. This is unlike you, not to want adventure!'

'Maybe I am becoming old and set in my ways.'

'Never! You will think about it, won't you? Your parents would enjoy travelling with you.'

'It seems that I must go. I will look at the information and ask the children if they would like to join me. Where are you sending us?'

'I wanted it to be a surprise; but if you prefer to look at the brochure, then you may. You used to enjoy spontaneity, Hope. It will be a memorable journey!'

Hope returned to her wreaths and was pleased with the results. She was also glad that it was settled that they would be staying in Yorkshire. Beaumont had been very generous with his offer of a holiday. The more she considered it, the more excited she became. Spending time with Mama and Papa was always a pleasure. A telephone conversation had elicited that her parents would be spending Christmas with Constance in London, but then they would travel on to Yorkshire for the new year.

There was great excitement in the house, as this would be the first time the Beaumonts had spent Christmas there together. Hope wanted it to be a happy occasion for everyone, especially Clarence.

She wrapped herself up warmly and ventured into the garden. Clarence was sawing logs, but paused as he saw her and waved. They sat together on a sturdy log, and Hope complimented him on the large pile of wood he'd already cut.

'Can't run out in this weather. Father used to make sure we were always warm.' He blinked and looked away.

Hope patted his arm. 'Your father was a good man.' She waited a little longer before saying, 'We must make Christmas as happy as we can. What shall we do about a tree? You're the expert, so may I leave it to you?'

'I've seen one that would do. It's on the way to the mill from the garden. Does that land belong to you? I wouldn't want to join old Potter in jail for chopping down someone else's tree.'

'Oh, Clarence, you are a joy. And yes, that land is ours, so do what you wish.' Hope shivered and got up. 'I'm going back to the house. Please don't stay out and get too cold.'

Already the young man was back at work on the logs.

* * *

Hope studied the contents of the packet Beaumont had given her. It was a very detailed itinerary of a luxurious-looking holiday. She called for the children. Ophelia and George quickly joined her. Impatient to impart her news, she said, 'I wish Clarence would hurry up.'

'He's a working man, Mama,' protested Ophelia.

'I know.' Hope smiled. 'It's just that I have something to tell you all.'

After Clarence had joined them, she explained about the holiday and that they would travel with her parents. She was amazed at their lack of enthusiasm. 'Ophelia, don't you want to go?'

'Is Papa going? I wouldn't want to leave him on his own.'

'He won't be on his own,' said Hope in despair. 'He'll have all the household servants, and the workers at the mill, and Robert, and anyone else we know here. What about you, George?'

'It sounds nice ...' George trailed off.

"Nice' — is that all you can say? It's perfect! And you, Clarence; what about you?'

'Me?' asked Clarence, looking bewildered. 'Why would you include me in your holiday plans?'

'Because you are part of the family. I thought we could *all* go.' She looked at the three blank faces and decided it was not a good idea to push things further. 'Very well. I am sorry to have interrupted your activities. Off you go.'

She sat on her own, flicking through the brochure once again, then she placed it in a drawer in the sideboard and tried to put the holiday to the back of her mind.

'You look upset, Hope. What's happened?' Beaumont entered the room and put his arms around her.

'Nothing, my darling, everything's fine.' Hope didn't want her husband to know that his present had been met with such indifference by the children. 'But what are you doing home at this hour?'

'I have something I need to work on and wanted to do it in the privacy of our home rather than at the mill. Also, I received some news this morning which you will be interested in. Sidney Potter has admitted to damaging the machinery at the mill in order to get William to go there, and he has provided a motive for his behaviour. Apparently he has a long-standing love of gambling, and used the proceeds of theft from my mill to buy stylish clothes in order to enter the gambling houses, as well as risk obscene amounts of money.'

'I noticed his clothes when Edna and I saw him in the pub. He seemed quite out of place. I am glad he has chosen to confess to everything. But I don't want to think of him now. I am determined we shall all have a happy Christmas together. Clarence has already chosen a tree to bring in. And now I want to prepare for your Christmas surprise. You must excuse me.'

Hope hurried off and threw on a coat, hat, and gloves before heading to the back of the house where the chauffeur was waiting for her with the motorcar. 'Let's get started,' she said as she climbed into the driving seat.

★   ★   ★

Hope felt cheerful as they walked back from the Christmas service at the village church. Clarence had been upset, no doubt recalling past Christmases with his father. Now he and Beaumont were walking together talking about changes they wanted to make in the garden.

For some reason, Ophelia and George were discussing their futures. Hope eavesdropped.

'I have told you before, George, I wish to be a doctor.'

'Maybe Clarence won't let you.'

'What's it got to do with him?'

'He'll ask you to marry him when he's old enough. Even Mama said he's fond of you.'

'I said he was fond of both of you,' Hope butted in. 'What are you going to do, George?'

'I still want to join Papa in the mill and

take over when he retires. I will be able
to do it now that I am strong. Watch me
run.' He raced ahead of them, catching
up with his father and Clarence.

'Oh, Mama, he will make himself ill
again. He is the most difficult patient.'

'I thought your father's suggestion
would be good for him. He has improved
greatly since we moved here, but a long
holiday would be ideal. I know you don't
like to be parted from him, so we must
all go.'

'All except Papa. And Clarence. *He*
doesn't want to go either. I agree with
you it would do George good: but I
am torn between spending time with
my grandparents and you and George,
and staying here to care for Papa and
Clarence.'

'It will be an adventure.'

'I am willing to help you persuade
George to go with you, but please let me
stay at home.' Ophelia suddenly darted
forward, crying, 'I knew it!'

They caught up with George, who
was sitting on the ground taking rasping

breaths. Beaumont was kneeling beside him, his hand on his shoulder.

'I think Clarence and I can carry you the rest of the way.' As they lifted George, Hope could see a look of defiance in his eyes. He couldn't speak, but she knew how much he detested his illness.

Back at the house, Nanny Swift quickly assessed the situation and ordered Beaumont and Clarence to lay George on the sofa in the sitting room. She gently raised his head on cushions and sent Ophelia for his medicine. 'You'll be better soon, George. Try to take slow breaths. I know it's difficult, but it has always worked before.' She ran a hand gently down his arm and he appeared to calm a little.

Hope sat on the floor at George's feet and waited. Poor child. He was battling against himself all the time. When would he be free of this wretched illness and be able to lead a normal life? Then she thought of Tobias Smith's sick wife, and desperately wanted to do something to help.

'I feel better, Mama,' whispered George. 'Ophelia told me not to run.' He looked at his sister. 'You were right.'

'I know.' Ophelia grinned. She grasped his hand, and Hope's heart melted at the sight of the two of them so closely bound.

★ ★ ★

When George was feeling strong enough, they all sat around the table and enjoyed a delicious Christmas meal.

'This beef is very tender,' declared Beaumont, accepting a second helping. 'I shall have to send our compliments to the cook.'

'Will the servants eat the same food as us?' asked Clarence, his mouth bulging with roast potatoes. He swallowed quickly. 'Sorry, I didn't mean to be rude.'

'The servants have exactly the same food as we do, don't they, Papa?' stated Ophelia. 'Only they have to wait until we've finished.'

'In that case, we'd better let Clarence carry on; he's doing a good job of being

178

the first to finish!' laughed Hope. She looked around at her family, and felt a warm glow of pride.

They all cried out in delight when a large platter containing the Christmas plum pudding was brought in, and enjoyed hearty helpings.

'I shall have to loosen my jacket,' said Beaumont, doing just that. 'What about you, George? Are you enjoying the meal?'

'I am, yes. It's delicious, but I think I've had plenty now.'

Hope noticed he was still a little pale, even though his breathing had eased considerably. 'If the others will excuse us, we can go into the drawing room if you like.' She winked at him.

They went along the hall, and when Hope opened the door, George gasped in delight. 'Mama, it's beautiful.'

Hope was pleased she'd put in the effort to decorate the large tree Clarence had cut and placed in a corner of the room. The ornaments sparkled as a weak sun danced in through the windows. Gaily wrapped gifts were set beneath the tree, and the smell of pine was intoxicating. The fire roared in the grate, and the garlands she'd made festooned the mantel.

'Christmas is a special time of year, isn't it, George? Now, what shall we do while we wait for the others to come along?'

'Mama, I feel I'm a disappointment to you in many ways. I thought I was well again, but I'm not very sensible, am I?' He pulled a face and continued, 'It would be wonderful to go on a voyage with you, but what would happen if I became sick? I would hinder everyone!'

'Is that why you're reluctant to come?' Hope was horrified and relieved at the same time. 'We can always take an extra bottle of medicine, and you could promise not to run too fast.'

George chuckled and hugged her.

★ ★ ★

Hope had insisted that Beaumont and the children put on their outdoor coats to wait on the front drive. She'd said she wanted to give him his Christmas gift.

180

What could it possibly be?

'Look, Papa!' Ophelia grabbed his arm and pointed. Coming round the corner at a reckless speed was his precious Rolls Royce, his one extravagance. It pulled to a sudden stop in front of them, and there was Hope sitting in the front seat, a big grin on her face.

'Come on, everyone; hop in and we'll go for a drive.'

'Drive?' questioned Beaumont. 'But you can't drive.'

'Yes, I can!' declared Hope. 'I have been instructed by the chauffeur. I kept it a secret.'

As the children clambered into the back, he sat beside Hope, who leant across and kissed him. 'Happy Christmas, Beaumont. Sit back and enjoy yourself.'

He soon got used to Hope's jerky gear changes and sudden stops, and enjoyed listening to the children's cries of delight. They headed out of the main gates and through the village before taking a road across the moor. At the highest point, Hope stopped the motorcar and pointed out the view.

'God's own country,' Beaumont said.

'It's beautiful, isn't it?'

'I never thought I'd hear you say that, Hope. You never cease to amaze me. Secretly learning to drive *and* calling Yorkshire beautiful!'

'I want to learn,' George said.

'Me too,' added Ophelia.

'I'll teach you all — you too, Clarence, if you like,' Hope offered.

'Not in this motorcar, you won't. You three can learn in the Austin.'

'Thank you, Papa. Let's sing carols on the way back,' Ophelia suggested.

Beaumont joined in the singing, and as they turned through the gates into the drive, the first few snowflakes of the winter drifted down.

* * *

On their return to Moorcliff Edge, Beaumont revealed *his* surprise. 'We've all had a marvellous Christmas Day, and this evening I thought we should think about those less fortunate. I have made a list of people connected to the mill with sickness in the family. I have asked the servants to gather together items of food from the kitchen store cupboard, and also clothes which are now too small for you children. Perhaps you and Nanny Swift could sort out the toys you no longer play with. We must ensure that the gifts are appropriate for the family, so please look at the ages of the children before packing the box.'

'But Papa, you told me the other day that some people can't afford medicine; if there is a sick person in the family, how will a toy or two help them?'

Beaumont was pleased with his daughter's thoughtfulness. She was very like her mother. 'I have spoken to the doctor and told him I will pay for any medicines needed. I have prepared cards to that effect which will be placed in each box.'

'They may not be able to read,' said Ophelia.

'Many of them have attended the classes we set up, but when we deliver the boxes we can explain.'

The children were soon busy sorting through the items and discussing what might be suitable for each family. Amidst the bustle, Beaumont paused and surveyed the scene. He and Hope should be proud to have such a united family. As he looked around, he caught Hope's eye, and knew her thoughts were running on similar lines. After a difficult patch, they were close again. He was grateful for all the Christmas gifts he'd received, but to be standing near the woman he loved and surrounded by his enchanting children, he felt he was the luckiest man alive.

10

Hope lay next to her sleeping husband and wondered how she was going to survive the weeks away from him. But she couldn't help feeling ripples of excitement inside her as she thought of the approaching holiday. It had been settled that it would be Hope, her parents, and George who would be travelling.

For a long while, Hope had deliberated about taking a servant with them. Florence was her first choice, as she could attend to George should he become unwell. However, the nanny had expressed an aversion to travel, and that had ended that idea.

Beside her, Beaumont stirred, put his arms around her, and pulled her to him. 'I would happily stay with you all day, Hope. Shall I play truant?'

'Yes, Beaumont, I think you should.' She snuggled beside him. 'But I know you won't.' She felt his body shake with silent laughter, and smiled. 'And now to serious matters. Florence will remain at Moorcliff Edge while we are away, so you will not have to worry about the welfare of Ophelia and Clarence. But who will come with us to attend me, Mama, and George?'

'Molly. You should take *her*. She has known George since he was a baby, and she is your lady's maid.'

'You are clever, my darling. I was also thinking about how I shall occupy myself during quiet times when I'm away. I have decided to resurrect my writing.'

'And what will you write about?'

'I shall write a book set in the future, where women have the vote and lead the country with sensible solutions to the problems they face in their lives.' Although she'd only voiced it light-heartedly, Hope wondered if such writing could be a possibility.

'I look forward to reading it. In the meantime, let's make the most of our time together before you pack your bags and leave me.'

* ⋆ ⋆ ⋆

Hope waited for the Austin to be brought round to the drive. As she took in the beauty around her, she wondered if she was doing the right thing in going away at this time of year. Long-ago planted bulbs were surfacing and smiling at the sun, and the myriad colours of spring lifted her spirit even higher. She would like to paint a picture of it.

George and Clarence were chattering away, Hope was pleased to note. Ophelia moved closer to her mother. 'I shall miss you,' she said, sliding her hand into her mama's. 'I should like to go to the school at the mill when you're away — I mean, as a sort of teacher. I am well-qualified for that, don't you think? I can read and write, and I believe I have a way of explaining things clearly to people who cannot quite grasp them alone.'

'I think that's an admirable idea, Ophelia. But I thought you wanted to be a doctor, rather than a teacher.' Hope spoke lightly, concerned that her daughter always occupied herself with the serious side of life — unlike George and Clarence, who were now hooting with laughter.

'I shall have to find something to fill the gap while George is away.' She turned away, but not before Hope saw tears glittering on her daughter's cheeks.

'My darling, you must not be upset. I have no doubt George will write to you. We shall be back before you know it, and your papa is delighted you will be here when he comes home from work.'

Ophelia wiped at her eyes and looked up at her mother. 'Really? Is that what he said?'

Hope nodded. 'Yes, he did. Now, here's the motorcar.' The chauffeur stepped out of the vehicle and held the door open. Hope raised her voice and asked, 'Who's going to be the first in the driving seat today?'

'Me,' cried Clarence, taking them all by surprise as he bolted to the motorcar and jumped in the front seat. 'Hurry up, let's go!'

As she sat in the back seat, bumping along the uneven road, Hope reflected on all that had happened since they'd arrived at Moorcliff Edge. Already she was thinking of Clarence as her son. He would look out for Ophelia, and perhaps pass on to her a lighter approach to life.

'My turn, my turn,' yelled George. 'Come on, Clarence, pull over.'

'Ladies first,' replied Clarence, braking hard, turning round and grinning at the two in the back. 'Ophelia, would you like to motor now?'

'No, let George. He can't seem to contain his enthusiasm. He will have another attack if he goes on yelling like that.' She let out a giggle, which was so unlike her that the others looked amazed.

George scrabbled into the driving seat and headed off at a top speed of ten miles an hour, with Hope begging him to slow down. He let out whoops of happiness as they sped along, and Hope couldn't get cross with him.

The journey home was much more sedate when first Ophelia and then Hope took the wheel. As she pulled up outside Moorcliff Edge, Hope said, 'That was fun. Thank you all for a lovely time. Will you inform the chauffeur that the motorcar can be returned to the old stables? I must go and see to household things.' She pulled a face, which had the children laughing, and went indoors.

★   ★   ★

On the day of departure, everyone gathered at the front of the house to wave off the travellers.

'I think I am as excited as George,' Hope said to Beaumont. 'I can't thank you enough for suggesting this. I will be eternally grateful.'

'Thank me on your return. Maybe it won't live up to your expectations. Have you heard George's chatter? He is very proud to be going on an adventure.'

'It will do him the world of good. You must take care of Ophelia and Clarence. And yourself. I do wish you were coming with us.'

190

'We will be fine, although it will be quiet without you.'

Hope was just about to get in the motorcar when she spotted a group of people heading down the drive. 'What's going on?'

'I have no idea, but it looks like Robert and a few other workers from the mill.' As the group drew closer, Beaumont went to meet them. 'Clarence! They are here to speak to you.'

Clarence stepped forward with George and Ophelia on either side.

Robert cleared his throat. 'Everyone at the mill wants you to know how much we respected your father. For a short time, some of us believed he brought his death on himself by drinking, and we want to apologise for that. Your father once told me you wanted a bicycle, and he said he was going to get you one for Christmas. We decided to club together to buy you one. It has taken a while, and is somewhat late for a Christmas present. We beg your forgiveness for thinking ill of your father. He was a fine man.' The group parted and a man wheeled a bicycle forward.

'Thank you, thank you,' was all Clarence said, but it was clear how moved he was.

'You must be going, or you will miss the train.' Beaumont hurried Hope, George and Molly into the motorcar.

They set off down the drive and Hope turned to wave at the large group of people watching them depart.

'Look, Mama, Clarence is following us.' George pointed excitedly.

Clarence pedalled frantically to keep up with them. He had a huge grin on his face.

★   ★   ★

The train journey to London seemed never-ending to Hope, although George's excited chatter relieved the tedium somewhat. After meeting up with her parents and spending a night in London, they set off by train again for Southampton.

'How far is it, Mama?' George had his face glued to the windowpane of the carriage and pointed out things as they passed. 'This is very exciting. I think I could be an engine driver rather than run the mill.'

'We're going to have fun with George to entertain us, Hope,' said Prudence quietly.

'This will be good for him, I feel sure. I thank Beaumont for arranging it, and you and Papa for accompanying us. I thought we might see you rarely when we first moved to Yorkshire. It seemed like the other side of the world.'

'From what you say, it has proved to be a good thing.'

'Oh yes, definitely. I can't think why Beaumont didn't suggest it before.' She laughed at her mother's raised eyebrows. Then she was surprised when Prudence moved closer to her.

'Hope, my darling,' she whispered, 'you have a look about you. Are you harbouring a secret?'

Hope was shocked. How could her mother possibly know? She herself had only found out a few days previously. She'd spent a sleepless night worrying that the voyage might be too arduous for someone in her condition. Then she realised she would be able to relax and be waited on completely on her holiday aboard ship.

Knowing there was no way of getting out of Prudence's direct question, she answered, 'Yes, Mama, I am, and that's precisely what it is — a secret.' Hope hugged it to her and thought of the letter she'd written to her darling Beaumont only the previous evening. She could have laughed aloud with happiness, and couldn't wait to return to Moorcliff Edge and be with him. But in the meantime, there was much to enjoy. She turned to Molly. 'Are you all right?'

'Oh yes, I am. It's strange hurrying along like this, but I like it. I must confess, I am a little anxious about how I will get on when I have to be separated from you.' She bit her bottom lip.

'We will spend as much time together as possible, Molly. But I am sure you will make new friends; there are bound to be ladies' maids by the dozen.'

Molly looked relieved, and followed George's instructions to look at the country-side as it flashed by.

When the train stopped, they climbed down onto the platform, and Herbert summoned a porter for their luggage and a Hackney carriage to take them to their destination.

'I'm looking forward to my holiday, Mama,' said George, walking alongside Hope and his grandparents. 'I must write to Ophelia and let her know all that she is missing. It would have been nice for her to come along, but she did say I should try and do more things on my own now.'

'We'll have a lovely time,' said Prudence. 'I shall paint your picture, George, and Ophelia will be green with envy when you tell her of your adventures.'

Hope slowed her pace and looked behind her. 'Molly, come and walk with us.'

The maid smiled and walked along beside George. Suddenly, he stopped and said, 'Look, Mama. Is that our ship?'

Hope squinted into the sunlight. 'I

195

can't make out the name on the side. Can you read it for me, George?'

The five of them stood still and waited for George's reply.

'Yes, Mama. It says, *Titanic*.'

PART TWO

1

Ophelia watched her father place a vase of daffodils by the headstone and stand for a few moments, head bowed. He often came to the churchyard to visit George's grave.

'Papa, I saw you leaving the house and followed you. Do you mind?' she said.

'I am pleased to have your company, Ophelia.' He took her warm hand in his cold one.

'Papa, I worry about you. Since ... since the tragedy, you appear broken. You have lost still more weight, and look quite ill.'

'I have told you before, not only do I mourn our loved ones, but I am riven by guilt for sending them on that ill-fated ship. I can't sleep, I can't concentrate on my work. There is so much to do. We are working at full capacity producing cloth for uniforms, and we are losing our workforce day by day. We hear too much bad news. Young men losing their lives. What will become of us all?'

Ophelia wanted her strong papa back. Since the news had reached them of the sinking of the *Titanic* and the loss of their family, he had changed. His body had become thin and angular, and he rarely smiled. He scarcely took time to tidy his hair, which was unkempt and flecked with grey. If Mama could see him now, what would she say?

Ophelia felt her face grow hot when she remembered her mother was no longer with them. At just fourteen, she had been forced to take on impossible responsibilities. She wouldn't have managed without Nanny's support over the last four years.

'We can't even visit your mother's grave. Where is she? Why did *she* die when other women were saved? It is intolerable not knowing what happened to her.'

'Papa, we *do* know what happened, she drowned. Why she wasn't in a life-boat, we'll never know. Knowing Mama, she was probably putting others before

herself. We should be proud of her.'
Ophelia couldn't count the times she
had endured this conversation. 'What
we *do* know is that Mama would want us
to live our lives to the full. That is what
I tell myself when I am feeling sad.' She
looked at her twin's grave. 'Poor George;
if he hadn't been poorly, he might have
survived the rescue.'

'And the baby ...'

'Papa, please, don't torture yourself.'

'I have the letter; here, see.' Her father
pulled a crumpled sheet from his pocket.
'I know it off by heart. 'My darling
Beaumont, I have wonderful news for you
and have decided to write before we set
sail. We are going to have another child.
Do not worry, I will take the opportunity
to rest while on board.' Another child,
Ophelia!'

She felt like crying. It seemed that she
and Clarence were of no account in her
father's eyes. He was too consumed by
grief for his two dead children to consider
the living. She was used to it now. She
thanked God she had decided to remain

at Moorcliff Edge rather than go with Mama and George. Without her and Clarence, Papa would have lost his mind completely.

Ophelia left her father poring over the letter. At times, she felt she was as confused as him. Clarence was the only person who understood what she was: a young woman of eighteen with a vocation she could no longer follow, and responsibilities she had no wish to have.

'Clarence, oh Clarence.' She almost wept when she found him weeding the flowerbeds near the house.

He threw down his trowel and caught her hand. 'Has he been at it again? I told you to ignore him. I love him like a father, but he's intolerable at the moment. Despite what Beaumont says, the mill is working at half-capacity because he's no longer contacting suppliers. He's deluding himself that everything's fine. If Robert hadn't been called up, it would have been all right, but there is no one to replace him. And the way your father treats you is insufferable.' Clarence pressed her lightly to him and whispered, 'I hate to see you like this, Ophelia. Let me speak to him.'

'No!' She pushed him away. 'I know I get cross with him; but he needs compassion, Clarence, and I don't think you'd give it to him, the mood you're in.'

Clarence grinned at her. 'You know me well, and you're right. I think it's time you enjoyed yourself, Ophelia. Would you care to help me weed the garden?'

She giggled and picked up the trowel, spraying freshly-turned earth over his shirt, before gathering up her skirts and running to the house.

In her room, she sank onto the bed and wondered what her future held. Her aspirations of becoming a doctor had been thwarted. As had her dreams of teaching. Since the start of the war, the mill library and school had been overlooked. She'd had no option but to care for her father, who had been almost insane with grief after the loss of her mother, her twin brother, and her grandparents.

George's loss was still as raw for her as the day she'd heard. He was half of her, she was half of him, and she would never escape the agony of being parted from him forever. It was as if her very skin had been peeled away and exposed to the elements. Clarence was a comfort, and she loved him dearly — she dared not say *like a brother*, for her feelings ran along different lines — but he was a mainstay, and for that she was grateful.

There was a knock on the door. 'Come in,' she called. 'Oh, Nanny, I'm delighted to see you. Papa is in a particularly black mood. Surely after all this time he should try to find a sparkle of sunlight in the darkness.'

Florence sat on a chair by Ophelia's bed. 'When something tragic happens, it affects people in different ways, my dear. Some deny the event and carry on as usual, while many go to the other extreme and end up like your father. I know of nothing to pull him out of his melancholy.'

'Sorry, Nanny, I was being selfish. You came to see me. What can I do for you?' Although Nanny Swift had asked her to call her Florence, Ophelia preferred the title; somehow, it comforted her.

'I wondered if we might go to the library at the mill. There are several books on the shelves here which we could exchange for the ones there. It would give the readers some variety.'

'What a good idea.' Ophelia jumped off the bed and headed for the door. 'We can also have a look at the mill and see how things are getting on.'

★   ★   ★

The machinery was running noisily, but the workers looked disenchanted. Most of the men had gone to the Front, and the women had enough worries to depress them.

'Hello,' said Ophelia cheerfully to the first woman she encountered. 'You are working hard as usual.'

The woman just sniffed at her and turned back to her loom. Then, suddenly, she rounded on her and asked, 'When is someone going to take responsibility?

It's chaos down here, not knowing what we're supposed to be doing half the time. It's not the same as when Robert Latimer and William Kenworthy were in charge. We need the work to feed our families. There used to be a nice atmosphere here, but it's not good anymore.'

That decided Ophelia. 'Nanny, do you mind if I join you later? I have something I must do.'

She rushed from the mill to the church-yard and found her father still keening over the grave. 'Papa,' she whispered. 'I need you to listen to me. Can you do that, please?'

His eyes met hers blankly, and he blinked into the sunlight. 'Ophelia? Is that you?'

She sat down on the grass next to him. 'Yes, Papa. Will you come to the mill with me?'

'The mill.' Beaumont struggled to his feet. 'Yes, of course. Is there trouble?'

'Yes, there is, and they are asking for your guidance.' Ophelia realised no one had actually said that to him before. They had been so filled with deference to his grief that they hadn't been able to tell him. Perhaps this direct approach would work. She desperately hoped so.

Taking Ophelia's hand, Beaumont strode towards the mill. 'Do you think Hope would mind if I spent some of my time working? I feel she wants me to be at George's graveside to watch over him.'

'Papa, dearest, I know Mama is watching over George, so it's all right. I promise.' Ophelia felt tears prick her eyes as she thought of the two of them.

'I love your Mama even though she's no longer with us, Ophelia.'

'I love her as well, Papa, and I love you. But we must think about the mill now. It is an essential supplier of soldiers' uniforms. It's important for the war effort. We must do some work in the office, and then speak to the employees.'

★   ★   ★

Beaumont sat at his desk and stared at the papers spread out before him. 'We need more modern machinery,' he said.

Ophelia was pleased. Her father was taking an interest in the business. Perhaps everything would be all right now. 'How do we go about that, Papa?'

'I'll get William to see what's available, and he and I can go and look at some.' He beamed at his daughter. 'Will you ask him to come and see me?'

Ophelia's heart fell as she realised her father was still stuck in the past. 'Oh, Papa, William has ... left us. Don't you remember? Robert Latimer was the manager after him, but he went off to fight.' She decided to leave out the episode with Sidney Potter, as that would surely complicate things further. Father was very delicate. 'Shall I deal with the order? Or will you?'

'Oh, you do it.' Beaumont slumped in his chair and closed his eyes.

Ophelia sat on the opposite side of the desk and sorted through the papers. She formed a half-picture of the workings of the mill, but not enough to feel properly informed as to what needed to be done.

Hastily tucking the relevant documents into a drawer, she went to find Clarence.

He was still weeding the beds, and looked hot and tired. 'Two visits in one morning? Not that I'm complaining,' he said as Ophelia charged towards him.

'I need advice,' she explained. 'Do you know anything about how the mill operates?'

Clarence blew out his cheeks. 'A bit. Father didn't go into the finer details, but he did outline things to me when he came home from work. It was a long time ago, though, Ophelia. Why do you ask?'

She told him about her father asking her to take charge. 'What am I going to do?'

'Give me half an hour to wash and change, and I'll accompany you to the office. We'll see what we can come up with together, shall we?' He looked questioningly at Ophelia, who nodded her head enthusiastically.

★   ★   ★

Ophelia walked slowly, as Clarence was still troubled by his leg wound. She couldn't abide the thought that he would soon be recovered enough to go back to the trenches. 'If you took control of the mill, Clarence, you wouldn't have to go back.'

'As you well know, I want to go back to do my duty. Our friends and neighbours are fighting for our king and country, and I want to join them. I know very little about the mill; and anyway, it's your father's responsibility. I do, though, have an idea to help his recovery. We will go to see my little secret as soon as we are finished at the mill. I hope you'll approve.'

Ophelia couldn't help skipping ahead of him. She turned, held out her hand, and waited for him to catch up and clasp it. 'I'm going to miss you. It was dreadful when you were away before. A gloom descended over us. Papa was full of dread that you wouldn't return.'

'He is a changed man from the old Beaumont.'

'I have a feeling that if he was his old

self, he would be thinking of other ways to help the war effort. I thought I should set something up.' Ophelia wondered what Clarence would make of her plan. 'It was having you back here and nursing you that made me think of it. Other big houses are being used for housing convalescing soldiers. I thought we could turn Moorcliff Edge into an auxiliary hospital.'

'I am quite sure you would manage it with Nanny's help, and also the Red Cross's. My only concern is that you will be surrounded by handsome soldiers who all want you as their sweetheart. You will forget all about me.'

Ophelia knew he was teasing her, but also that there was an element of genuine jealousy in what he said. Since his return he had made known his feelings for her.

There was no sign of Papa in the office, but Clarence explained everything he knew to her. After half an hour, Ophelia felt exhausted. 'It's so dry and complicated. The best thing would be to get Papa back. Please, let's go and see this secret you were talking about. I can't look at these papers any longer.'

'We're going to Moorcliff Farm,' Clarence declared.

★ ★ ★

'They're through here.' The farmer's wife led the way to an outbuilding where they were greeted by a black Labrador. 'This is the mother; the father is a spaniel. He's out in the fields with my husband. We've got three bitches and three dogs to choose from.'

As they entered the barn, the mother dog growled at Clarence. 'She's all right with me here, but she wouldn't care for a stranger coming in on their own and handling her puppies. She doesn't seem to mind you, though,' she said, smiling at Ophelia.

Ophelia knelt down in the straw and picked up one of the plump, cuddly bundles. 'Oh, they are lovely. Shall we have them all?'

'That'd be a lot of work!'

'You think it's a good idea, then, to get

one for your father? He'd have to care for it, wouldn't he?' Clarence asked.

'Not necessarily. He could leave it for me or one of the others.'

'Would you like a male or female? These are the girls.' The woman pointed out three of the puppies.

'I think we'll have a female.' Ophelia looked over at Clarence, who nodded his agreement. 'How do we choose?' she asked the woman.

'What sort of nature would you like? These two are quiet, and this is the noisy one.'

'We'll have the noisy one. Papa will have to take some notice of her, surely. She's so pretty, with her black coat and white patch above her nose.'

'They'll be ready to leave their mother in two weeks. Come back then.'

'I can't wait!' As soon as she'd said it, Ophelia glanced at Clarence. By that time, he would already be on his way back to France.

As they left the farm, Ophelia said, 'Clarence, you are very thoughtful. You have enough troubles of your own, yet you concern yourself with Papa's welfare and the mill. I will miss you greatly when you go.' She linked her arm through his, and together they slowly made their way back to Moorcliff Edge.

'I'll miss you, too, Ophelia. You are very dear to me, as I expect you know. Beaumont and your mother did a very noble thing by taking me into your family. I felt loved. And you and George were especially valuable to me, as I could be myself with you both. I would do anything for you and Beaumont.' Clarence stopped and picked up a stout stick from the ground. 'Will you write to me, Ophelia? Draw me a picture of the puppy, and tell me what is happening at Moorcliff Edge?'

'Of course, Clarence,' she replied.

'And one more thing.' He grinned his cheeky grin and said, 'Race you back!' He loped off with an ungainly gait, the stick lurching wildly as he threw himself forward.

'I'll be the winner,' Ophelia shouted.

On reaching Moorcliff Edge first,

Ophelia immediately realised she had left Nanny Swift in the library at the mill. Cursing her forgetfulness, she was about to go back to apologise when she saw Papa and Nanny coming across the lawn.

'Nanny,' called Ophelia, 'how can you ever forgive me? Clarence waylaid me and I forgot to let you know we were leaving. I am sorry.'

When Florence reached Ophelia, she whispered, 'I found your father wandering around the mill. He was talking to the workers, but he seemed disorientated, so I took him out into the fresh air.'

Ophelia nodded. 'That was good of you. He's not at all well, but Clarence and I might have something which will help in two weeks.' She let out a laugh. 'You'll like it, too, Nanny, I feel sure.'

A shout made the two women look up. It was Clarence. 'How dare you treat a wounded soldier in that way? You should have let me win. I'll report you, and you'll have your rations cut.' He wielded his stick above his head.

Unperturbed, Ophelia said, 'All right, Clarence, I know it's time for luncheon. Come on, let's all go indoors.'

2

Time passed quickly, and soon it was the morning of Clarence's departure. Ophelia carefully selected her outfit to see him off. She chose an emerald-green silk dress from the back of the wardrobe, and held it against her as she looked into the mirror. A pale-cheeked young lady looked back, with dark, auburn-tinted hair elegantly piled up in ringlets on her head. Slipping into the dress, she pushed a stray hair behind her ear and hurried down to see Clarence.

He looked smart in his uniform, and Ophelia caught her breath. It would have been so easy to fall in love with him; he was handsome, dependable, funny, and a dear person. She opened her arms to him and they embraced. Eventually, Ophelia drew away, with tears in her eyes and sadness in her heart.

Clarence kissed her lightly. 'Goodbye,

my dear Ophelia. Take care of yourself and your father. I will be thinking of you.'

Ophelia ran to her room and sobbed into her pillow. What if she never saw Clarence again? He wasn't in the best condition to fight, his movements were slow, and she was frightened for him. All the men who fought in this war were brave; most of them had been willing volunteers, and there were a lot of young men who'd given no thought to their own survival. They'd sacrifice their lives for their country.

Nanny Swift knocked on Ophelia's door. 'My dear, I'm here because I knew you'd be sad for Clarence.' She sat on the bed next to Ophelia and smoothed her hair.

After a few minutes, Ophelia struggled upright. 'How is Papa? I haven't seen him this morning.'

'Clarence said goodbye to him, but I don't think Mr Beaumont realised he was off to war again. Do you feel strong enough to talk to your father now? Should we try to persuade him to go to the mill each day?' Nanny was picking at the folds of the bedcover. 'I want him to be well, as I know you do. How can we help him? It's been a long time since you lost your dear mother and brother.'

Ophelia sighed. 'We must inspire him with new interests. Let me tell you about my plans for the house.'

★ ★ ★

When Ophelia came back from the farm, she knew to look for her father in the churchyard. 'Papa, look what I've brought for you. A present.' She held the warm bundle out to him to take. 'I've christened her Faith, but she's only had that name for a very short time, so you may rename her.'

'Faith?'

'Take her, Papa.' Beaumont held out his hand, and the puppy licked it and struggled to escape from Ophelia's grasp. 'I can't hold her any longer, Papa, please take her.'

Beaumont clutched the puppy against

219

his coat. 'There, there, Faith, we don't want to drop you. Who do you say she belongs to?'

'She's yours now, and will need to be looked after and trained. In time, Faith will accompany you when you go to work at the mill. She will be a good companion if you treat her properly.'

'I had a dog when I was a boy, long before I met your mama. I trained him, too. He was a faithful companion. Come along, Ophelia, we must find some dishes and suitable food and a nice place for her to sleep.'

Ophelia happily followed her father's instructions as they sorted out everything necessary for the new member of the household. Nanny was amazed when she came into the sitting room to find Beaumont lying on the floor with Faith climbing all over him, nibbling and licking his face.

'May I ask what's going on?'

'This is Faith, Florence. She is a new member of the ... of the family. Yes, that's right. She will keep me company.'

While Beaumont played with Faith, the two women talked quietly by the window.

'I have received a letter.' Ophelia patted her pocket. 'Remember how I told you about the hospital I want to set up here? Well, everything is going to plan, and we should be able to go ahead soon.'

'That is very good news, but is your papa aware of what is about to happen to his home?'

'I have told him and been met with a blank gaze. I think if we wait a couple of days I may well be able to gain his full attention. He is already much more his old self. Look, he is smiling.'

'And what if he doesn't agree?'

'He'll agree. It is just the sort of benevolent gesture he and Mama would have made. I feel as though everything will begin to improve now. Let us pray the war will soon be over and everyone will return safely.' As she said it, she knew her prayers could not be answered. Every week they received news of the loss of another man from the village. Her heart went out to their families. She almost wished Clarence would be wounded again so that he could come back to safety. He had only been gone a short time, but she missed him dreadfully.

It was as though Nanny could read her thoughts. 'We must make up a parcel for Clarence. Cook has started knitting socks and we must all write letters. I will describe the garden.'

'And I will tell him about Faith. She was his idea, and he will be delighted to know that Papa likes her.'

★ ★ ★

Gradually things began to change at Moorcliff Edge. Beaumont became less agitated. He fussed over Faith as if she were a newborn child. He spoke to her in whispers, as if telling her secrets. Ophelia noticed he didn't visit George's grave as often. Faith was a devoted companion, and the two seemed besotted with each other.

Ophelia had despatched one of the few remaining servants to the village to send off the parcel they had prepared for

Clarence. Everyone in the household had contributed something. Even the puppy had licked the picture Ophelia had drawn of her. It was not a great likeness, for she was not an artist like her grandmama or even her mother, but she knew Clarence would like to know Beaumont had a companion.

As she thought about friendships, Ophelia couldn't help thinking of Edna, who had been distraught about Hope and Molly. She had known them for many years and was very close to them both. Now, as Ophelia walked to the library at the mill, she wondered if she would see Edna today.

Fortuitously, they both entered the library at the same time. 'Edna, I was just thinking of you. How are you?'

'I'm well, thank you. How is Mr Beaumont progressing? I see he's taken to coming to the mill almost every day now. The feeling among the workers is much more positive.'

'You must have seen him with his dog. She's called Faith. He adores her.'

Edna laughed. 'They haven't gone unnoticed. The children would love a dog, but I have enough to do. Which reminds me, I came in for some books for the children. I must continue to encourage their love of reading. Your mother taught me to read and write. She taught Molly, too.' Edna's voice broke and she gave a little cough. Ophelia saw the glitter of tears in her eyes.

'Mama was a born teacher. And you are, too, Edna: teaching your own children. They are able to write to their father. Their letters will cheer him until he comes back safely.' She bent forward to hug her mother's dear friend, who gripped her tightly.

Sniffing, Edna sat at the table. 'Since you told us about the house becoming an auxiliary hospital, I was wondering if I could be considered to work there. As a volunteer, I mean; I would like to continue my paid employment, as we need the money. But I would also like to help the soldiers. If they're all as dear as Thomas and Clarence, it would be an honour.'

'What a very gracious thought. We'll talk again when things are more settled. There's a lot to organise. I suppose I'd better get back, but I wanted to take a few of the books for the hospital library, for the use of the patients. Don't worry, I won't leave this one with empty shelves.'

Depositing the books in the hall of her home, she went in search of her father. He was not at George's graveside, so she walked to the end of the garden and scanned the horizon. She thought she saw him walking with Faith and ran towards them.

'Papa, Papa,' she called, 'wait for me.'

Her father didn't respond, but Faith did. The puppy stopped, and Ophelia thought she saw her ears prick up. Then she barked until Beaumont stopped and looked around him. When he caught sight of his daughter, he waved and walked towards her. 'Ophelia, have you decided to walk with us?'

Ophelia sank down onto the grass and caught her breath. 'Father, I need to talk to you. Come and sit with me.'

Faith scrabbled over and licked Ophelia's hand. 'Yes, Faith, I love you, too. You're a dear girl, but please stop washing me.' She tried again with her father. 'Please come and sit with me, Father.'

'When you call me that, I am either in trouble, or you want something.' Beaumont smiled at his daughter.

'Well, Papa, you are right. But you are not in trouble. We have no manager at the mill. I know you've been going there, but you must use a bit more authority. The workers need someone to look up to. You could take Faith with you.'

Beaumont stood with his eyes half-closed. Then he said, 'William isn't with us now, and Robert has gone to war.' He raised a hand to his forehead and rubbed it, frowning as he did so. 'We are at war?'

'Yes, Papa,' answered Ophelia. Poor man, he was still finding things difficult, but he was trying extremely hard. Her heart wrenched as she watched him.

'What about Clarence? He should have the position. Yes, that's it, Clarence.'

'No, Papa, Clarence has gone to war, too.'

Beaumont landed at her side with a thud. 'Ophelia, I am struggling to remember things. Your mama and her parents died, and so did George — I know that's right, but then everything is such a blur. My mind clears when I'm on the moor with Faith. I trust you completely, my darling daughter. I will do as you say.' He hugged her tightly. 'Don't leave me, Ophelia.'

★ ★ ★

'It is good to hear your voice, Great-Aunt Constance. I am sorry we are unable to visit you, but it is very difficult here with Papa being as he is. He is a little better since I last spoke to you, but struggling still. He looks less tired and thin.' Ophelia paused to listen to her aunt at the other end of the telephone. 'James Henderson? I have no idea who he is. He married Isabella Padstock? Ah, the Padstocks are very rich, I remember. He

227

is going to visit us? But why? And with his son?'

After the conversation ended, Ophelia sank into an armchair. This was too much. She couldn't entertain strangers, not with Papa still fraught. And she was too busy with the mill and the hospital to spare any time. Why were they coming? Aunt Constance hadn't explained the purpose of their visit, as she'd been too caught up in describing how the war was affecting London. All Ophelia knew was that the Hendersons would be arriving at Moorcliff Edge shortly.

$$\star \quad \star \quad \star$$

It became clear on the day of their arrival.

'I am James Henderson and this is my son, Lemuel. You must be the daughter — Olivia, isn't it?'

'I am Ophelia.' She took an instant dislike to the Honourable James Henderson, who explained how he was involved in the organisation of the auxiliary hospitals. He looked much older than her father.

228

He was plump and balding with a few wisps of hair.

'And where is Plantagenet, may I ask?' He chuckled.

Ophelia was shocked. Her father hated his Christian name. She had never heard anyone use it before. 'Please be kind to Papa. He has suffered greatly from the loss of Mama and my brother George.'

'We will treat him well,' Lemuel assured her. There was a gentleness about him which Ophelia immediately liked. How could the son be so different from his arrogant father? She found herself admiring Lemuel's good looks. His hair was the colour of honey. It appeared as if he had tried to tame it, but a tuft stood up above one ear, which made him even more appealing. He flashed her a dazzling smile, and she almost lost his next words as she grew fascinated by his indigo-blue eyes. 'Father, you have told me you knew Beaumont well when you were younger,' he said.

'I am not sure 'well' is the correct word. I knew him, but he was a strange man. Always wanting to help the poor. He captured Hope's heart. I'm still not quite certain how, as she is ... was an intelligent woman. So, where is he?'

'Out on the moors, walking with Faith.'

'A new wife!'

'Faith is his dog,' Ophelia explained. 'She has helped him recover ... a little, at least.'

'Father would probably like to rest and have some refreshments, but if it is acceptable to you, I would very much like some fresh air. May we seek out your father?'

Lemuel had an easy manner, and the two young people found plenty to talk about as they made their way along a path through the bracken. 'I am sorry about my father's behaviour. I think this work has changed him somewhat. He is full of his own sense of importance. He is not a bad man, and you will find plenty to like about him as you get to know him.'

'I am sure that will be the case,' Ophelia lied. 'What about you, Lemuel? You work with your father?'

'I am helping him as there is so much to do. If you are wondering why I haven't gone to fight, it is because I am in a reserved occupation.'

Or maybe your father has pulled some strings to keep you from the war, Ophelia thought, knowing she was being uncharitable. 'I can't imagine what it is like over there. I don't *want* to imagine it.' As they reached the brow of a hill she stopped and looked around. 'There is no sign of Papa. I expect he has already gone home via a different route, so let us return as well. You must be tired and hungry after your journey.'

The walk back to Moorcliff Edge was a pleasure for Ophelia. She missed Clarence's easy chatter, but Lemuel was an entertaining companion. Then the house came into sight and Ophelia saw her papa and Faith entering the front door. She hoped that James Henderson would not be cruel to him.

'Papa,' she called, rather breathless from hurrying Lemuel along. 'We have visitors.' She caught up with him in the hall, and Faith nuzzled her lightly. 'It's James Henderson. A friend of yours, Great-Aunt Constance said. Do you remember I told you he was coming?'

'And I am Lemuel, his son.' Lemuel stepped forward with his hand outstretched. 'I am pleased to make your acquaintance, sir.'

An awkward silence ensued until Beaumont smiled and took the proffered hand in his. 'Do call me Beaumont. James Henderson? The name seems familiar. Come, let us see what he wants with us, shall we, Faith?' He strode into the drawing room and frowned at the man before him. 'Ophelia tells me you are James Henderson. I knew a Henderson once, but it was a long time ago. Married a charming lady called Isabella.'

'That's right, Plantagenet. Nothing wrong with your memory. I am here to help with the setting up of an auxiliary hospital.'

Ophelia moved nearer to her dear papa as she feared he would not be able to handle the situation. 'Shall we go to the dining room? I have asked cook to prepare an early luncheon for us all.' As she led the way along the hallway, she whispered to Beaumont, 'Do you *really* remember him? Or are you just pretending?' To her great surprise and delight, her father grinned broadly and winked at her, just before taking his place at the head of the table.

The conversation was involved, and Ophelia tried her best to follow everything that was said, but it was useless. 'Are we to leave the organisation to you?' she asked.

James Henderson nodded. 'Yes, that's right. You show us the space available and we will outline how best to use it.'

'Of course, you and your father will be able to put forward your ideas,' said Lemuel.

'I am grateful for that,' said Beaumont. 'We have quite a lot of ideas, and I wouldn't want anyone riding roughshod over them. Is that clear?'

He looked quite ferocious, but Ophelia had to put a hand to her mouth to hide a smile. It looked as if this visit was proving to be good for her papa. But how long would he be able to keep it up?

After they'd eaten, Beaumont took them around the house and, with Ophelia's help, he told them of the space they were prepared to allocate to the hospital. Lemuel nodded and smiled a lot, but his father looked grim during the entire tour.

'What a splendid house you have, Beaumont. And delightful and charming company,' said Lemuel.

'Do you mean the dog, or my daughter?'

Lemuel laughed. 'Both, yes indeed, both.' He bent to stroke the puppy who seemed pleased at the extra attention she was getting.

Beaumont nodded and pulled out a watch from his pocket. 'I am due at the mill. It's essential work, as I'm sure you are aware. Ophelia will, of course, accompany me. You are both welcome to rest here until our return. Please excuse us now.'

Surprised, Ophelia followed her father from the house. When they were sufficiently out of earshot, she said, 'Papa, you were wonderful. Has everything returned to you?' She caught his arm and looked up at him. Then a shiver of despondency passed through her as she saw tears in his eyes. 'What is it, Papa? Please tell me.'

'I remember him. I didn't like him then, and I don't like him now. I don't want him interfering with our house. How dare he call me 'Plantagenet'! I'm sure he only did it to annoy me. I remember another meal we shared. It was a dinner party at Constance's, and your mama arranged to give food parcels to the poor. That was the very moment I fell in love with her.' He rubbed at his eyes and continued walking. Ophelia had to almost run to keep up with him. 'I will make sure the mill is looked after, and that the hospital goes ahead, but I think we can do so without much interference from James Henderson, don't you, Ophelia? Please help me.'

Thinking that it would be nice to be

without James Henderson, and less nice to be without Lemuel, she reluctantly agreed. If only there were a way to keep the younger man at Moorcliff Edge a little while longer.

3

'I think we are ready, Ophelia,' Lemuel said.

'Just as well, as the first patients are expected to arrive this morning. I am glad we have inspected everything, but I still find it strange there are so many people living in our house.' Ophelia collapsed into an armchair. 'I feel exhausted, but I am very happy we are able to help the wounded soldiers.' She was surprised to see Edna entering the room. 'Edna! What are you up to? I must say, you do look very smart in your uniform.'

'Matron said I could bring you some tea. She said you've been working too hard and she doesn't want extra patients. So, tea and biscuits for two.'

'That's very kind, thank you. Do you like working for her?'

'She expects a lot from us, but she's fair and compassionate. I'd better be getting back as we still have some beds to make.'

Lemuel sipped his tea. 'Your father is making good progress, I feel. From what you've told me about his lack of interest in the mill after the tragedy, he is quite changed. I believe he spends most days there.'

'He certainly goes most days, and he is managing the mill well. But he often sneaks away to walk Faith on the moor. I don't blame him. It was your father's arrival which precipitated the change in him. They've never liked each other, and something snapped in Papa on that day you arrived.'

'Father can be difficult, and I won't excuse him. Perhaps it was just as well he was called away to the hospital at Swindale Hall.'

'Bigger and better, I expect.' Ophelia put a hand to her mouth. She didn't mean to be unkind about his father. 'Lemuel, I have been meaning to ask you something. Your name is unusual. Why did your parents choose it?'

'It's simple. My mother was reading

Gulliver's Travels — the main character is called Lemuel — and she decided to name her first son after him. Your father has an unusual Christian name too.'

'I suggest you never call him 'Plantagenet'. At no time does he ever use his Christian name! He prefers to be plain Beaumont. He doesn't have a title like your father.'

'He is an interesting man.' Lemuel paused. 'Listen. I can hear some vehicles approaching the house.'

Ophelia jumped up and ran to the window. She held out her hand to Lemuel. 'Come here! Look! The first of our patients have arrived.'

The couple stood hand in hand for some time as they watched the wounded men being brought into Moorcliff Edge.

Ophelia felt Lemuel's grip tighten. 'That has decided me. Whatever Father says or thinks, I am no longer prepared to sit on the sidelines. I am going to enlist.'

There was no time for Ophelia to reply, or even to think about what Lemuel had said. Edna came hurrying into the room and requested that they come to the wards. It felt strange for Ophelia to be walking through the recently rearranged rooms of her own home. She had become used to the house since they'd moved north, and their London residence had become a dim memory. The sitting room and drawing room each had eight beds. She had insisted that the coverlets be cheerful — much to the annoyance of James Henderson — but luckily he had left Moorcliff Edge, and Lemuel had agreed with her decision. Beside each bed was a chair with a colourful cushion. As Ophelia watched the men being helped — and, in some cases, carried — to their beds, she wondered if the feminine touches she'd suggested would even be noticed. Now it was clear to her that what they required most was rest and recuperation, not a fashionable place to live.

'Miss Beaumont, when we have settled our men in, I will introduce you to them if you wish,' Matron said, with pursed lips.

Ophelia hid a smile; she knew she was being dismissed. She respected the matron who was in charge of these soldiers, but she would not like to do anything which would result in getting on the wrong side of her. From the corner of her eye, she spotted Edna tending a young man. He appeared upset and buried his face in the pillow. Edna whispered something to him and gently patted his back. The gesture took Ophelia's mind back to George, and how she and Mama had tried to console him when he was unwell. A lump came to her throat and grief overcame her like a tidal wave. If she became emotional, she would be of no use to the patients. She hurried from the room.

A couple of smaller rooms had been designated as family ones, and Ophelia sat in an armchair, staring out of the window. The late spring bluebells swayed in the gentle breeze, but even so, the garden had taken on a slightly desolate look since Clarence had left. He would have known how Ophelia was feeling without being told; now there was no one to whom she could be as close.

'I understand it is a very emotional time for you, Ophelia.' Lemuel had followed her and now stood at her side, his hand lightly on her shoulder. 'We can have no concept of the suffering these men and others like them are enduring. It is truly humbling.'

Although he hadn't *quite* understood her inner feelings, Ophelia felt lifted to know he had taken the trouble to follow her and offer comfort of a sort. Perhaps she was wrong to believe she couldn't be attached to anyone other than Clarence.

★   ★   ★

The day before Lemuel's departure for London, he suggested to Ophelia that they take a walk on the moor.

'I shall remember this day when I am in France. I will summon up a picture of the landscape with beautiful Ophelia in the centre.' He took her hand as they walked along, their bodies close.

Their friendship had developed into something more, and they had often taken walks together, or sat in the garden confiding in each other. Sharing kisses had become natural. There was nothing about Lemuel you couldn't like. Being with him was so very pleasant.

'I wish you wouldn't go. I can't bear it. Why did you volunteer?'

'What would you have thought of me if I hadn't?'

'Don't you dare blame me. I don't want you to go. I've lost too many loved ones. I don't want to lose another.'

'Aha, I am glad you said that. I spoke to your father last night after dinner. I told him that I loved you and said I believed you felt the same about me; and so ...' He paused and took a deep breath. '... I asked for your hand in marriage.'

Ophelia gasped. 'What did he say?'

'He said he approved, but he wouldn't make you do anything you didn't want to do. He also told me how much he loved your mother.'

'I do love you, Lemuel.' She wondered

if she was telling the truth. Was she saying it so that he could leave happily? She didn't know, she was confused.

'You'll say yes?'

'Yes, I say yes.' She smiled at her fiancé, but her thoughts were of Clarence.

★ ★ ★

'Miss Beaumont, come and change my bandage. I recognise your footsteps and know you're near.' The blind soldier smiled as he held out his hand for her to take.

'John, you know full well I am not allowed to change your bandage. You'll get me in trouble with Matron, and you'll be in trouble with Papa if he catches you holding my hand.' Ophelia's heart went out to the young man. She didn't mind the flirting as long as the men were cheerful. It was the quiet ones mired in the depths of despair that she felt worst for. There seemed to be no way she could help them.

In her pocket were the two most recent

letters from Lemuel and Clarence. Her heart leapt when she thought of Clarence, but thinking about her fiancé made it plummet. It had been a huge mistake accepting Lemuel's proposal. She had grown fond of him when they worked together organising the hospital, and he was a kind, gentle man, but they had little in common. There wasn't the laughter she'd shared with Clarence. Bu there was nothing that could be done. When he returned, they would be married. She couldn't break off the engagement as she'd given her word. A soldier had enough to endure without the addition of a broken heart. She would pretend he was her heart's desire, even to Papa.

Having made her way into the garden, she wandered to the herbaceous border, knelt down, and pulled the letters from her pocket.

My dearest Ophelia,
I hope you are in good health and Beaumont is too.

All is well here. We made another successful advance and will attack again in a few hours, hence this brief letter. It is wet, muddy, and noisy, but you mustn't worry. I will be fine, and soon return to Moorcliff Edge and you. There are things I should have told you before I left.

You would like the horses here. I wonder how the puppy is.

Much love, Clarence

The letter made Ophelia feel better. She held it against her cheek and imagined it was Clarence who was close to her. Then she remembered Lemuel's letter and puffed out her cheeks. There was no time to re-read that one; she had to get back to the house now, or taste Matron's wrath.

★　★　★

'Miss Beaumont, I am pleased you are a good timekeeper. I need someone to assist me with a dressing. Follow me and

246

do as I say.'

'Yes, Matron,' whispered Ophelia, trailing after her. For all her strictness, Matron worked hard for those in her care.

When they had washed their hands, Matron pushed the dressing trolley to a bedside. It was Sergeant Tom Harris's bandages they would be changing. Ophelia smiled at him and, as he grinned back, she saw the pallor of his face. As Matron peeled the soiled bandages from his torso, Ophelia had to clench her jaw to prevent herself from flinching. His wounds were deep and jagged. Fresh blood seeped from them as soon as the pressure bandages were taken off and the packing removed from the deep cavities in his chest. Automatically, her hand reached for his, and he gripped it tightly.

With clean dressings and the promise of a cup of tea, Tom lay back on his bed, his eyes closed.

'That will be more comfortable for you,' said Ophelia.

'Yes, it will. Thank you,' was all he said.

She wheeled the dirty dressings to a

side room where she disposed of them and carefully washed the trolley down. A voice made her jump. 'You did well, Ophelia. I think you are a born nurse.' It was Matron.

'I wanted to be a doctor, but that was before … well, it was a while ago; and then the war began and things took their own direction.'

'There will still be time when the war is over. Never give up your dreams.' Matron sailed away to tend to another patient, leaving Ophelia reeling. Would she really be able to fulfil her aspirations? And, if so, what exactly were they? Going about her duties that afternoon, she listed them in her head while the soldiers flirted with her and she returned their light-hearted repartee.

But as soon as she was free to leave, she changed from her uniform into a light cotton dress and went up to the moor. As she walked, she realised why her father came here so often. The openness allowed her to clear her mind and focus on what needed to be sorted out. At the top of her list was her engagement to Lemuel. She had promised to marry him, but only because she felt she had to. It must be the war which had had such an impact on her; everything seemed so urgent. Given more time, she would have asked Lemuel to wait until his return for her answer; but she hadn't, and now she would be tied to him for life.

Ophelia reached a vantage point and was able to look down at Moorcliff Edge. Seeing the area where Mama had taken them driving caused her to shiver with sorrow. Mama had been such fun, and George had tried very hard to do things despite his poor health, and Clarence? Well, Clarence had endeared himself to them all. And she missed him with all her heart.

* * *

'Ah, my dear Ophelia, come and eat. We have much to see to.'

'What do you mean, Papa?'

'It is a surprise for you, although I expect you to help. Your mama used to assist me.' He absentmindedly held a scrap of meat out for Faith.

'Papa! You are not to feed Faith at the table. She mustn't learn to beg.' Ophelia knew her father would say nothing further. He often withdrew into a dream world when he thought of her mother. She would have to wait and see what was expected of her. Since Nanny Swift had felt compelled to do more for the war effort and had left the area to work in a munitions factory, Ophelia had felt weighed down by the responsibility of ensuring Papa was functioning properly. He and Faith still often disappeared to the moor for hours on end, whatever the weather. It was always a relief when he was in one of his better moods and would converse with her.

At meals Ophelia did her best to engage him in conversation, even if it was totally one-sided. 'When I came back from my walk the patients seemed unsettled. There was a feeling of excitement about them. Is that something to do with you, Papa?' She paused. 'This food is good, don't you think? As you know, I asked cook to give us the same meals as everyone else. She does well producing delicious repasts from very few ingredients. You should tell her.' There was still no response. 'I received a letter from Clarence. He asked after Faith. If you remember, it was his idea to get you a puppy.'

'Have you heard from Lemuel?'

'Yes, Papa, I have. He is well, but longing to return so that we … may be married.'

'He's a good man. Now, hurry up, Ophelia, we must start soon.'

Ophelia left her food unfinished and rushed after her father who was already half-way to the door. As soon as they entered the drawing room, she realised what was going on. Some of the beds had been pushed to one side, and others were in a row with their occupants facing one end of the room. Those men able to leave their beds were sitting on chairs. Papa's precious magic lantern was on a table in the middle of the room.

'The piano, Ophelia. The sheet music

is there.'

'Oh, Papa, you might have warned me so that I could have practised!' Ophelia felt overwhelmed at the thought of having to perform in front of an audience; it was a long time since she'd played.

'Don't fuss. These men need entertaining. We must do our best for them.'

Deciding that she must do just that, Ophelia put her heart and soul into the music. She wasn't as accomplished as her mother had been, but the audience didn't appear to mind the occasional wrong note. Although their faces couldn't be seen in the dark, it was obvious from their laughter and comments that the men were enjoying the show. Beaumont inserted the painted slides into the lantern, which magnified them onto the screen in front of the audience.

For the grand finale he showed one of his favourites, 'The Ratcatcher'. The audience laughed loudly when the rat disappeared into the sleeping man's mouth.

Even Ophelia was laughing, although she'd seen the magic lantern shows many times before. 'The Ratcatcher' had been one of George's favourites. As she thought of her dear brother, she was amazed to find her throat didn't constrict with searing grief; she felt happy with her memories.

Then she remembered John. He wouldn't have been able to see a thing. Poor man. How could she have been so insensitive as to have ignored his obvious needs? So much for Matron's praise. Rapidly, she brought her fingers down on the final chord and left her seat at the piano.

John was sitting next to Tom, and they were laughing and chatting together. 'Ah, it's Miss Beaumont,' said John. 'I recognised your footsteps. I thoroughly enjoyed your piano playing, and Tom here gave me a running commentary on the pictures.'

Ophelia felt like hugging both the men, but now was not the right time. It was inspiring to see them helping each other. She hoped that Clarence had a companion like that wherever he was. Then she wondered why her first thought hadn't been for her fiancé.

'Refreshments will be served in a short while. Just let me put my equipment away,' said Beaumont. 'Come on, Faith, you'll have to move.'

John instinctively put out his hand and the dog nestled against him. 'I have a dog at home,' he said. 'He's called Blackie.'

'This one's a girl, and her name is Faith,' said Ophelia. 'She belongs to Papa. He takes her for long walks up on the moor.'

'I'd like to do that,' said Tom, 'but I doubt if Matron would let me go far, for fear of busting my wound open again.'

'You could sit in the garden with Faith; or there are some more dogs down at the farm.' Ophelia wondered if she'd said too much; they could be overrun with animals. Luckily, Edna and another volunteer arrived with sandwiches and a tray of cold drinks.

'If I told you this was beer, would you believe me?' Tom asked John. 'After all, you can't see what it is, can you?'

'I can smell it, though,' grinned John.

'And you shouldn't make fun of a blind man.'

Ophelia could feel the camaraderie and was grateful her father had put on the show. It had done wonders for the men's morale — this pair's and, judging by the laughter around her, everyone else's.

At the far end of the room, she spotted Matron and went over to her. 'Did you manage to see any of the slides?' she asked.

'I did. And I would like a word with your father. Can you tell me where he is?' Matron looked stern, but then she usually did. Ophelia was a little worried. Was she going to chastise Papa?

'He's putting the magic lantern away, but he'll be back in a short while. Can I get you a sandwich?'

Then Beaumont entered the room and Matron strode towards him. The two huddled in a conversation which Ophelia couldn't hear. At last, Matron left the room, and Beaumont helped himself to a sandwich which he proceeded to share with Faith.

'It was a grand show, Beaumont. Have you any more slides? Or we could have a piano recital!' The men continued chatting with Beaumont, and he seemed content in their company. Ophelia sat on the piano stool and watched him. She had been trying to rouse him from his slough of despond for so long that she had sometimes wondered if anything would ever change.

'Matron had a word with me,' Beaumont said to Ophelia, leaning against the piano.

'Are you in trouble?' She smiled up at him.

'No, I'm not. I'm in favour! She wants me to give another show. She said my — I mean, *our* — performance was magnificent.' He puffed his chest out and his lips curled up in the smile Ophelia remembered from long ago.

4

Beaumont and Ophelia sat in the garden, with Faith bounding around chasing butterflies. It was an idyllic morning.

Beaumont sifted through the morning post and frowned at one of the envelopes. 'This one looks official; it must be for the army people.' He turned it over in his hands. 'It's addressed to me, though. I'd better open it.' As he tore at the sealed strip, he laughed at the antics of the dog who was running round in circles, chasing her tail. With the page spread out before him, he turned his attention to it. His heart lurched and missed a beat. 'No, I will not believe it. It cannot be true.'

'Papa, what does the letter say?' Ophelia leapt from her chair to her father's side. 'Please, Papa, what is it?'

With difficulty, Beaumont formed his words, 'It would appear that Clarence is missing. My dear, it's terrible news. Just

257

like last time.'

Ophelia dropped to her knees beside him as she whispered, 'Please tell me it isn't so, Papa. I love Clarence. I love him far more than Lemuel. It is Clarence who holds my heart.'

★　★　★

The weeks dragged by as autumn set in. Ophelia did her duty and always put on a cheerful face when working at the hospital, but inside she felt wretched. She had no one to talk to. When Nanny Swift had left, she'd wished her well and promised to keep in touch, but that separation had been yet another loss. Somehow, over time, their letters to each other had become less frequent. Edna was kind, but Ophelia didn't feel she could unburden herself to her. Papa had once again plummeted into gloom, and the mill was being neglected as he spent almost every day out on the moor with Faith. There was no way Ophelia could see to the mill as well as her duties in the hospital. She didn't know what would become of the business. She folded sheets automatically, trying not to picture Clarence's sweet face.

'Ophelia, I need a word.'

'Yes, Matron, how may I help?'

'It is you who needs help. I have watched you since you heard the news about your friend, and I am worried for you.' Ophelia was surprised when Matron took her hand and continued, 'I am going to give you some advice, whether you want it or not. You need to talk to someone about your loss and your father is that someone.'

'I can't weigh him down further. Have you seen him? He is just as he was after my mother's and brother's deaths. He hardly eats, I doubt he sleeps much, and he barely speaks.'

'Exactly. You are in the same position, as you both love Clarence. I was upstairs a short while ago, and your father was sitting at the escritoire in what I have been told was your mother's room. Go, now. That is an order.'

Ophelia made her way slowly up the

stairs to her mama's old rooms. Nothing had been changed since the tragedy. She knocked at the open door. 'May I come in, Papa?'

'Ah, Ophelia. I have found this hidden away at the back of a drawer. You must have it.' He held out a necklace.

'It was Mama's?'

'I gave it to her. It is a piece of suffragette jewellery. She was an active member of the movement. I didn't encourage her in it, though.' He let out a sob. 'I should have supported her.'

'Please don't be filled with remorse. Remember the happy times you shared. You would never have bought her such jewellery if you hadn't supported her, and she would have known that. I will wear it now. It's beautiful, and I shall treasure it.' She fastened the clasp of the necklace. 'Papa, I would like to walk with you and Faith. I need to tell you about my feelings.'

'It's no good having feelings. You need blankness to deal with grief. But Faith and I will walk with you, nevertheless.'

The dog was already on her feet, wagging her tail.

There was no chatter as they walked briskly over the moor behind the house. The air was damp and an autumnal chill seeped into Ophelia's bones. She took a deep breath. 'I loved Clarence. I am sure I feel about him as you did about Mama. I can't bear it, Papa. His loss is destroying me. I can barely get up. I have no appetite. I can't sleep.'

'But what about Lemuel?' her father asked. 'You are engaged to be married to him.'

'Papa, I am not sure I love him. He is attractive, and pleasant enough company, but he doesn't captivate me like Clarence. It's Clarence I love. I know it's wrong, but it seems to me I have nothing to live for now. Only you.'

'And I have only you, dear Ophelia.' He held her arm to stop her and they turned to face each other. 'I loved Clarence like a son. I have lost my wife and two sons, but you too have suffered greatly, and I will do everything in my power to make

261

you happy.'

As he spoke, Ophelia couldn't stifle a wail which echoed over the moorland.

★　★　★

Beaumont had no idea how he got himself and Ophelia back to Moorcliff Edge. He was shocked to the core; her howl of pain was as if she'd been sliced through. Even though he had told her it was no good having feelings, as he half-dragged her across the moor, his own sentiments churned through him. If Ophelia was going through half what he'd endured over the years since his darling Hope had died, then he had to help her. But he had no idea how.

Faith trotted along at his side, running around to be beside Ophelia from time to time. When they reached the house, John was sitting in the garden, muffled up with a scarf and hat. He rose as they approached. 'Beaumont, is that you?' He laughed. 'I can hear Faith.'

'Help me, man. Ophelia's unwell.'

John shambled towards him and felt for her arm, taking it and holding her firmly. 'It's all right, I've got you. Let's take you indoors.'

At the sound of his voice, Ophelia seemed to rally. Slowly they led her into the house. 'John, thank you. I felt unwell and Papa brought me home.' Then she sank onto a chair in the hall.

'I'll get Matron to see to her,' whispered John to Beaumont, who nodded.

Faith put her head in Ophelia's lap and whimpered. Distractedly, she gently patted the dog's head, murmuring to herself. Beaumont ran his hands over his face. He would *not* let Ophelia suffer anymore. He must find out the fate of their much-loved Clarence.

'Ophelia,' said Matron, 'you are to come with me.'

Obediently, she rose and followed the matron. Beaumont put a hand to his head and massaged his scalp, trying to work out what his first step should be. It was John who finally prompted the answer to that question. All he said was, 'Is there someone who can help you, Beaumont? Someone to get in touch with?'

Suddenly, he was on the alert. 'Yes, John, there is. I have to go to London. You will be in charge of Faith while I am gone. Do you understand?'

'Yes, sir,' he replied. 'I shall do a good job.' He stood ramrod-straight and moved closer to the dog, who brushed against his leg before sitting at his side.

'Of that, I have no doubt. I only wish I had as much confidence that *my* job will be executed as competently.'

Unhappy at the thought of leaving Ophelia, Beaumont was slightly cheered to see her sitting in her room with Matron, chatting quietly. Perhaps her demons would stay away. He explained he would be absent for a few days, and that John would be looking after Faith. She was to rest and do what Matron told her in order to be well again on his return. With a hug from his daughter and an encouraging smile from Matron, Beaumont packed a few things and departed for London.

'Beaumont, you must be frozen. Where's your coat?'

'What a lovely welcome, Constance!' Despite the journey and his anxiety, Beaumont couldn't help but laugh. He'd given Constance no warning of his arrival — there had been no time for that — but he knew she would welcome him and let him stay.

'How is Ophelia? Is she with you?'

'No, she is unwell.' Beaumont sat down without being asked and looked around him. Things looked just as they always did. The furniture hadn't been changed, and the paintings on the walls were as he remembered them. Sadness threatened to take hold of him, but he remained focused on Clarence, his reason for being there.

'Poor child. She's been through a lot — as have you, Beaumont. We have all lost someone dear, and it hurts, doesn't it?' They sat in silence for a while until

Constance added, 'James Henderson has told me all about the hospital at your Yorkshire house.'

'James Henderson! Huh,' groaned Beaumont, making Constance chuckle.

'You never did take to him, did you? His son's engaged to be married, did you know that?'

Beaumont knew of Constance's failing health, but he was surprised at the question. 'He's engaged to Ophelia.'

'*Ophelia?* Oh, yes, I remember now. You told me. Is that why you're here?' The colour on Constance's cheeks was high and she seemed flustered.

Beaumont felt it was time to change the subject. 'May I have some tea? You don't mind if I stay here for a few days, do you? I'm going to look up some old friends.'

★   ★   ★

Ophelia was feeling sad without Papa. She sat in Mama's room at the escritoire and looked around her. Was it her imagination, or did the room still smell of Mama's favourite rose perfume? She breathed in, longing to gain some comfort and strength from doing so. Since Papa had given her the suffragette necklace she had worn it every day. Yesterday John had heard it jangling and asked her about it. She'd described the white, green and purple hues of the necklace, and taken it off for him to hold and feel. Since Sergeant Tom, as she called him, had left Moorcliff Edge, John had been somewhat lonely. It had been a good idea of Papa's to put him in charge of Faith while he was away. The two of them were inseparable. The dog now appeared to regard John as her master. Ophelia couldn't help thinking that Papa was selfish to go to London for no obvious reason when so much needed doing in the house and at the mill. The army needed to be clothed, and with winter coming, the woollen fabric they produced was in great demand. They could barely keep up.

She went over to the wardrobe. With the door open, the scent of the clothes was strong. She grabbed a black and white woollen dress and held the material against her face. 'Oh, Mama, if only you were here.' What was she to do? Without Clarence in her life she was lost. Marrying Lemuel seemed intolerable. But she would do it. How did that compare to John's future without his sight? And the other men who had lost legs, or worse? She was lucky compared to them. She had all her senses, the love of her father, and would have a comfortable life. What more could she ask for?

She pulled a turquoise dress from the cupboard and slipped it off its hanger. It looked to be her size, so she decided to take it to her room and try it on. If it fitted, she would come back for other items of clothing. It would give her a feeling of closeness to her mama, and that was exactly what she needed.

Sitting at the escritoire again, she idly pulled out the drawers and glanced inside. A bundle of letters and a drawer full of diaries intrigued her. She longed to read them to find out more about her mother, her hopes and dreams, but knew it would be wrong to do so. They should be burnt. She would speak to Papa upon his return.

There was a knock at the open door. 'Faith brought me up here. I know I'm not really allowed, with it being upstairs, but I wanted to talk to you in private, like.'

'Come in, John. Make your way over to me and I'll help you find the chair. Here we are. Now, what is it you wanted to talk to me about?'

'I listen a lot, and I've heard you talk to Matron. I know about your friend being missing. I wanted to say how sorry I am. It's a rotten war. Whoever wins, both sides will be the losers. But you're not alone. We all know how it feels. Every one of us. I've lost mates, that many I can't count them. It stabs at me here.' He touched his chest.

Ophelia put her hand on his shoulder and he reached up to place his hand over hers.

'I'm leaving tomorrow. Going home. I'm not sure what my future holds, but I'll always remember you. You have been the brightness in my dark world, and I thank you for that.'

Ophelia couldn't speak.

'You'll have to see to Faith. She needs a master, but your father will be back soon, don't you worry.' He patted her hand.

'We must go to the farm, John. They couldn't find homes for all the puppies so they kept a couple. But now they are grown, the farmer is keen to find owners for them. Would you like one? Would your dog mind?'

'Blackie would be pleased to have a friend, just like the rest of us. I'd like to take a dog home with me, it will take the attention away from my difficulties.'

'Good. Take my arm and we'll go now.'

★   ★   ★

At the farm, the woman said, 'It's good to see you. How can I help you?'

'John is going home and he would like to take a dog with him. Would that be all right?' asked Ophelia.

'It would be perfect. As you know, we

270

still have two left here. They're both male, and we've named them. One is called Tommy, and the other Fred.'

'There's no contest then,' replied John. 'I would like Tommy. He will remind me of Tom who was my friend here. What's he like?'

'He's chocolate brown, with soulful eyes. Can you hear his tail thumping on the floor?' Ophelia watched as John and Tommy started to get to know each other. It seemed that by some innate instinct, Tommy knew John needed gentleness. Faith bounded around until it was time to go.

'He's taken to you already, John,' declared Ophelia. 'We'll have to sort out a lead for Tommy; there will be something at the house. You don't want him getting lost on your journey back home.'

'I'll miss you, Ophelia. You've been good to all of us. We often talk about you. Would you mind if I wrote to you? Well, I'd have to get someone else to write it, or you wouldn't be able to read it!'

'You're always cheerful, John, and

very positive. Do you really feel like that inside, or is it a bit of an act?' Ophelia was sure he wouldn't be offended by her direct question.

He shrugged. 'No point moping around. No one likes a moaner, do they? Just get on with what life dishes out, and be thankful you're still breathing, I say.'

By the time they'd reached Moorcliff Edge, Ophelia felt a bit more sanguine. Perhaps there was a small chance Clarence was alive, even a prisoner somewhere.

★   ★   ★

Ophelia tried hard to heed John's words. She had learnt much from his attitude to life. *No one likes a moaner,* she told herself; but she knew she didn't moan, keeping her thoughts very much to herself. *Just get on with what life dishes out, and be thankful you're still breathing.* At times she didn't feel thankful. Sometimes she wished she'd gone on the *Titanic* with Mama, George, and her grandparents, but she knew that was a stupid and selfish notion. It was just so hard to think that she might never see Clarence again.

Trying to concentrate on scrubbing the floor of the dining room, she was disturbed by shouts and cheers, apparently coming from the back of the house.

Matron bustled in. 'Those men! There'll be more injuries before the day's done.'

In spite of her words, Ophelia knew Matron was pleased about whatever was going on. 'I've finished the floor. May I go and see what the patients are up to?'

'You may. You can pick up the pieces.'

Ophelia left the house through the back door. It was strange how so much had changed in the past few years. At one time, she wouldn't have used any door apart from the front one. And as for scrubbing floors, even Mama with her forward-looking ways would never have done that, she was sure.

Outside were a crowd of men surrounding a patient with the use of only one arm. 'Come on, get on it — otherwise someone else will have your turn.'

It was good-natured, but she felt sorry for the man as he climbed on the bicycle and tottered off round the yard. She smiled, though, when she saw that he was grinning from ear to ear as the others cheered him on. And then she recognised the bicycle. It belonged to Clarence. Tears formed, and she could barely answer when she was asked what she thought of the man's skill at riding one-handed. 'You should have seen Alf — he's lost a leg and an arm, and he still did it!'

Thank goodness John was not there, otherwise he too would be on the bicycle, trying to cycle without being able to see. But he would have done it, of that she was sure. If only she had his attitude to misfortune. She stayed watching the antics of the men, although she could barely speak to them or raise a smile. When one of them appeared with a ball, they all rushed off for a game of football on the front lawn. The bicycle had been flung to the ground and forgotten. Ophelia picked it up, and as she held the handlebars she pictured the last time she'd seen Clarence riding it. He'd been returning from the village; and when he'd seen her, his face had lit up and he'd waved. She could picture his expression as if he were right there in front of her. A sob escaped her. More than anything, she wanted to feel close to him. Not caring what anyone thought, she flung her leg over the crosspiece, and pedalled away round to the front of the house and down the drive in an attempt to escape from her life at Moorcliff Edge — for a short time, at least.

She headed towards the village, needing to be among people who were living normal, everyday lives, not cooped up in the hospital with sick patients. She was determined to have some fresh air and company outside of the hospital environment.

She slowed as the houses came into view. Young children played outside even though it was chilly. They were calling to each other and laughing. Ophelia thought back to the enjoyable times she'd had with George, although they had hardly ever played outside due to his health. If only the wretched war would finish and she could train to be a doctor! It seemed her list of wants was never-ending.

A scream jerked her out of her reverie. She saw a little girl lying on the ground, her arm twisted beneath her. Women came running out of their houses, but no one appeared to know what to do. Ophelia dropped the bicycle and hurried over. After a brief examination, which she'd learned how to perform from watching Matron and the doctors, Ophelia took her scarf from her neck and made a sling for the child.

'You'll be all right,' she assured her. 'You're being very brave.' Ophelia was sure the young girl had a sprained wrist, but there were no broken bones. She comforted her and her mother.

'Thank you for looking after my daughter, Miss Beaumont. Would you like to come in for a cup of tea?'

Although it wasn't the entertainment Ophelia had been after, she readily agreed. Most of the neighbours squeezed into the tiny house along with them, and she was the centre of attention. She knew some of them from the mill, and chatted happily with them.

As she cycled back towards Moorcliff Edge, a chuckle escaped her as she realised she'd been running from injured people only to find an injured child in the village. She knew that John would have enjoyed the irony.

By the time she reached home, Ophelia was in a cheerful mood. The soldiers had gone inside, and she put the bicycle away carefully. When Clarence returned, he would want to ride it, she thought optimistically.

★   ★   ★

Beaumont set off early for his club. He had been away a long while, and it seemed strange to be walking through the streets of London after the openness of the landscape around Moorcliff Edge.

Stepping over rubble, and shocked at

the houses which had been demolished by the Zeppelin attack last September, he finally arrived at his club, pleased to see it was still standing.

'Beaumont! Where have you been hiding yourself?' was the first thing he heard as he walked through the door of the wood-panelled club room.

Smiling, he answered the question and sat at a table with the man, who he remembered as Anthony someone.

'Have a drink,' he said to the man. 'It's a bit early for me, but I'm here for information. I need to trace a member of my family who's missing in action.'

Anthony shook his head. 'I'll accept the offer of a drink, but I've no idea about procedure of that sort.' He thought for a moment, then added, 'He'll have to be matched up with his service records, won't he? You could try Perkins over there for a start. Don't expect a lot of him. One of his sons was killed recently.'

Beaumont nodded and approached Perkins. 'May I sit with you? My name is Beaumont. I used to frequent this club, but I haven't been here for a while.'

Perkins lifted his shoulders and returned to reading his newspaper. Feeling he was wasting his time with this man, but unsure where else he could go, Beaumont said, 'Please accept my condolences for your son's death. I have a son who I am trying to trace. He's missing in action, and I have no idea where to start looking for him. I do not like to intrude on your grief, but any help you could give me would be much appreciated.'

The silence that followed nearly tore Beaumont's taut nerves apart. Then Perkins said, 'I know your name. The mill owner. Lost your wife and child as well as her parents. I can give you an address, but don't be too optimistic.'

Resisting the temptation to snatch the piece of paper with the vital information on it and run out into the street, Beaumont continued to speak with Perkins for another half an hour as politeness dictated. Then he was free to continue his quest.

Expecting it to be just a short time

before he knew Clarence's fate, Beaumont became exasperated as one address led to another, until the trail ran dry. There was nothing else to do now except return to Constance. But first, he wanted to inspect his own London house.

Everything seemed to be as it had been left. Dust covered the surfaces and it had a musty smell about it. It would never be used by him now, so perhaps he should think about selling it, or at least letting it out to the auxiliary hospital commission. He supposed he would have to endure the company of James Henderson one more time.

Wearily, he approached Constance's house. The blackouts were at the windows, and he shivered at the starkness of the town he used to call home.

'Beaumont, you've been away all day and half of the evening. You'll wear yourself out. Tell me what you've been doing.' Constance sat on a sofa in her magnificent sitting room sipping a glass of sherry.

Running his hand through his hair, Beaumont poured a large glass of whisky from the decanter on the sideboard before flopping down in an armchair close to the fire. 'It's cold out there,' he said. 'Very well, Constance, I'll tell you. Clarence is missing in action and I am here to find out what happened to him.'

She smiled at him. 'I didn't really think you'd come all this way just to see me, Beaumont.'

'Sorry, that sounded rude. It's always delightful to see you, Constance, but ...' He had no time to tell her about Ophelia's feelings for Clarence, as they were interrupted by the arrival of a visitor.

'James,' said Constance, 'I'm pleased you were able to accept my invitation to join us this evening.'

Beaumont thought he would explode. Why on earth had Constance invited James to dinner when she knew how he felt about the man? He could only put it down to her confused state. Then he remembered his manners and stood up to shake hands with the despicable man in front of him who was destined to be Ophelia's father-in-law.

Beaumont had tired of James Henderson's company very quickly. They had all three dined together, and then Constance retired to bed, leaving him alone with the pompous man. There was nothing to say to him apart from enquire about Lemuel.

'He's doing well,' stated James. 'Of course, he's officer material and will be promoted quickly.'

Of course he will, thought Beaumont, uncharitably. Aloud, he said, 'That's good news. I expect you're proud of him.'

'Naturally. We are all proud of our families, are we not?'

Beaumont thought of his family. Most of them were dead. There was only Ophelia and Clarence now. Clarence! 'James,' he almost shouted, 'could you explain to me how one would go about finding a soldier missing in action?'

'That's easy enough. But I will need another glass of port.'

They settled themselves, and

Beaumont hung on every word he said.

It was the early hours of the morning before James Henderson left the house and Beaumont went to bed. He couldn't sleep with all the information he'd gleaned twirling around in his mind. Sitting at the desk in his room, he took out a sheet of paper from a drawer and started writing, wanting everything down in black and white so he could start tracing the whereabouts of Clarence. Even if he was dead, it would be better to know rather than wonder if he was suffering somewhere.

As he fiddled with his plate of bacon and kidneys the next morning at breakfast, he said, 'Constance, I shall be out for most of the day, but may I use your telephone first?'

The old lady arched an eyebrow. 'Are you at long last asking my permission to do something, Beaumont? You never have in the past.' She sipped her tea.

Grinning broadly, he said, 'You are right. But this is terribly important and I desperately want to get it right.'

'Of course you may use the telephone; and if I can help in any way, I shall do so. All you have to do is ask.' They continued breakfast in silence.

Constance left him alone and Beaumont started on the strategy he'd decided upon during the night. By lunchtime, he was hoarse with trying to explain things over the telephone, and his thoughts were becoming confused.

'Beaumont, you must take a respite. I can see you are caught up in something, but you need sustenance. I will not budge from your side until you agree to eat.'

'Constance, you are a wonder, do you know that?' He planted a kiss on her crepey cheek and led her into the dining room. 'You deserve an explanation.'

Over luncheon Beaumont disclosed his worry about Clarence. 'I hate to admit it, but Henderson was helpful last evening. He gave me a lot of information and people I could contact. But I have not moved further forward.'

'I have a friend I could speak to if you wish,' offered Constance.

5

'Will we be able to fulfil this latest order in time, Edna?' Ophelia slumped at Papa's desk in the office at the mill.

Edna turned from the filing cabinet and smiled. 'We can only do our best. Everyone is working flat out. I doubt even your father could get more out of the workers.' She walked over and placed her hand on Ophelia's shoulder. 'You look worn out. Are you sleeping?'

'Not well. I worry about Papa. Constance telephoned yesterday. Papa is staying with her, but he was out. She told me not to be concerned about him, as he is fine, but he has been terribly upset about Clarence.' Ophelia had no wish to speak or think about Clarence. Every thought of him being lost stabbed at her heart. 'I wish Papa would come home so that I can care for him. But what about you, Edna? Any news of Thomas?'

'You are just like your dear mama. You always think of other people. I am happy to tell you I received a letter from Thomas yesterday. He said the conditions are dreadful, but he is well and looking forward to coming home. I can't imagine when that will be. This war seems never-ending, and every day there is news of more death and injury.'

Ophelia knew numerous men from the village had been killed, and that the deaths blighted the lives of those left behind. She would try not to dwell on it. 'How are the children?'

'Just as children should be! Noisy and happy. They don't realise how serious the situation is. The girl from the village who looks after them when I'm working is marvellous, she is full of energy. I still regret giving up my voluntary work at the hospital, but when you said we needed to take charge of the mill, I knew I couldn't do everything well.'

'I too wish I was still able to help with the patients. Maybe when Papa comes back he will be able to take charge here again, and we can return to our duties at the hospital. Matron said only this morning how much she misses our help.'

'You have done the right thing. Morale was so low with no proper leadership, but now with you and me working together, the atmosphere has changed completely. And we must remember that *this* is important war work too. We are all doing our bit. Now, I must go and do my daily tour.'

When Edna walked out of the office, Faith left her position under the desk and stretched before approaching Ophelia. She bent down and stroked the dog's neck. 'You miss him dreadfully too, don't you? He'll come back, but what state he'll be in, I can't say. We'll have to look after him. And when I marry Lemuel and move away, it will all be up to you. No! I can't!' As the tears coursed down her face, Faith licked them away until Ophelia couldn't help but laugh. 'We'll go for a nice long walk later, I promise.'

★   ★   ★

Ophelia and Faith set off across the moor. It was chilly, but it felt good to breathe in the cool air after the stifling atmosphere at the mill.

Faith bounded off, stopping every now and then to investigate a rabbit hole. Then she changed direction and hared off again out of sight. Ophelia called to her, but she didn't appear. She was usually such an obedient dog. Ophelia called again, but still there was no sign of Faith. In desperation, she ploughed on through the damp bracken, and then she heard the dog barking. When she'd found her, Faith continued to bark and jump around Ophelia. 'What is it, girl?'

Then Ophelia looked towards the house, unable to believe what she saw. Were her eyes deceiving her? She was sure it was Papa. He wasn't alone, but was too far away to hear her, and she couldn't make out who he was with.

She made her way across the moorland back to the house with Faith by her side. In her haste, she tripped over a root and nearly fell to the ground. She took a deep breath and looked towards the house again, trying to identify the second figure; he looked familiar, but she couldn't believe her eyes. Reaching out for Faith, she whispered to her, 'Is that Clarence? Or am I dreaming?' Then she raised her voice and shouted, 'Let's find out!'

Together they raced towards the house, but by the time they reached it there was no sign of either man. Frustrated, Ophelia went inside and searched for Papa. He was not in their section of the house, and he wouldn't be in the rooms used by the hospital. It had been her imagination playing tricks. She had heard that it was possible when you wanted something very much.

Ophelia sank into a chair in the sitting room. Faith stretched out, her head on Ophelia's feet. It was very comfortable, and she felt her eyes closing as she dropped into sleep, her dreams troubled and full of Clarence appearing and disappearing.

★   ★   ★

Ophelia awoke with a start. At first she couldn't recollect where she was. Then she remembered and hauled herself out of the chair, disturbing a still-sleeping Faith. 'Sorry, girl,' she whispered. 'If only I had *really* seen Papa and Clarence! I think I'd better go to bed; I need to be fresh for work at the mill in the morning.'

But as soon as she lay down, images tumbled through her head and she was unable to sleep. She thought of Mama and George, and then Papa and Clarence. Her torment was unbelievably painful — but she was not the only one to have lost loved ones, she told herself sternly. She would concentrate on the mill: an important delivery was due in the morning, and Edna would need her to be at her best.

★ ★ ★

Ophelia wasn't hungry after her troubled night, but stumbled to the dining room. She knew the importance of food in order to build her strength for the day ahead.

She wondered if she was still asleep and dreaming when she heard, 'My dear Ophelia.'

'Papa!' Ophelia rushed into the room and hugged her father. 'You're back at last. I thought I saw you yesterday, then I couldn't find you, and thought my mind was playing tricks.'

'I did arrive yesterday.'

'Oh, why didn't you find me?' Ophelia felt disappointed that he'd chosen not to seek her out.

'I was occupied. I went to see Matron.'

'Are you not well?' Ophelia was immediately contrite.

'I am quite well. Now, sit down and have some breakfast. Cook has made my favourite, scrambled eggs and sausages.'

Ophelia was puzzled. Papa looked much better than when he'd left for London, and he seemed to be cheerful. Uninterested in the food, she looked around for Faith. Where was she? She almost always lay under the table during meals, and she should certainly be here now her master had returned.

'Do you know what's happened to Faith?' she asked her father.

'I believe Faith may have wandered onto the moor.' He was surprisingly calm.

'Father! She never goes alone.'

'Then you had better go and find her if you're feeling well enough. Go along. I'll talk to you later.'

Before going out, Ophelia slipped on some boots and grabbed a cloak. Once up on the moor behind the house, she stopped and looked about. Seeing no sign of the dog, she whistled and called. And then there was a noise behind her.

'Faith, good girl, come.' The dog's tail thumped against her leg as she made a fuss of her. 'Whatever is your master thinking, letting you go out on your own? And why did you leave him? You never leave his side.'

'Here, girl, leave the lady alone. Come.'

Ophelia recognised the voice immediately, and there before her was Clarence. She rushed forwards and hugged him. She was shocked when he pulled away.

'Hey, steady, what are you doing?' he asked.

'Clarence, I'm hugging you because I'm very pleased you are safely home.' She could see from his eyes that he didn't recognise her.

'You know my name. Who are you? Do I know you?'

Her feelings were mixed. Buoyant because he was home again, and sad because he wasn't the same man who had left. 'Let us walk towards Moorcliff Edge and I will tell you about myself and how you know me. May I take your arm, please?'

He held it out for her, and walking close together, they made their way back, with Ophelia telling him about his life before he'd left for the war.

As they reached the house, he said, 'I can remember some things. I remember a boy, my friend.'

'That was my brother George. He died when the ship he was on hit an iceberg.'

'The *Titanic*!'

'That's right.' Surely, if he remembered

George, he could remember her too. 'Look, Clarence, the herbaceous border. All dead at this time of year, and sadly neglected since you left.'

'I like gardening.'

'You do. Maybe in the spring you could work in the garden again.'

'That would be nice. You're nice too, very kind. Are you married?'

'I have a fiancé.' She didn't want to think of Lemuel. All she wanted was to be with Clarence.

'He's a lucky man.'

Ophelia couldn't agree. The woman Lemuel was engaged to be married to did not love him.

She knew what she must do. Now that Papa was back, she no longer needed to work at the mill. She would use all her time to show Clarence places he might recognise, and tell him about people he'd known and things he'd done. She didn't care how long it took, she would help him get his memory back. He needed her — but more than that, she needed him.

6

Ophelia was excited at having them both home safely, and listened to the details of how her father had traced Clarence. Constance's contact had been able to obtain Clarence's service record, which confirmed that he was not dead, but in London awaiting transfer to a hospital in Hampshire. Beaumont sought permission, as his guardian, to take him back to Yorkshire.

Every day since his return, Ophelia made sure there was a routine for Clarence. She had organised it as if it were a military operation. They all breakfasted together, and then Beaumont and Clarence walked around the grounds.

Ophelia talked with Matron and the doctors, trying to learn how best to help her dear Clarence. 'You are doing all the right things,' Matron assured her. 'We can think of nothing further. As far as we can all tell, it's a matter of time. He has suffered little physical injury, so a trauma must have occurred to lead to a blocking-out of mental pain. We often see it in the patients who are transferred here, but because we know nothing of their personal lives, we have no idea whether their memories are real or not. The doctors thought Clarence's memory would be triggered by seeing you. That's why your father suggested you join him on the moor. But he must be more shell-shocked than we originally thought.'

Ophelia had to be satisfied with that. When Clarence returned to the house, she talked to him about George and her mama, and things they'd done when they were all together, reminding him of happy times such as when they'd learnt to drive. She hesitated over reminding him of his father, but in the end she decided she should. 'Clarence, can you remember your father? He was called William Kenworthy and he was the manager of the mill here.'

'Is he still here? Or did he go to the

war?' Clarence looked animated as he questioned her.

'I am afraid to tell you he died in an accident before the war began. I'm sorry.'

'It's not your fault. Many people die.' Clarence stared straight through her. 'I saw a lot of death. My friends, they died. It was horrible.' He shook his head, and Ophelia wondered if he was trying to clear it of unbearable memories.

Wanting to give him something happy to think about, she said, 'Shall we go outside again? There's a bit of time before luncheon.' If she was lucky, her timing would be just right.

The men were again playing around with the bicycle. They greeted Clarence affably, although he barely knew them, as he hadn't been staying in the hospital accommodation. 'You look too fit to ride this cycle,' laughed one of the men.

Clarence went over and gripped the handlebars, squeezing the brakes and kicking at the pedals. 'I know this bike,' he said, with a grin appearing on his face. Ophelia held her breath. He hopped on it and sped away, ignoring the shouts from the other men.

'It's fine,' said Ophelia, 'he'll be back shortly. Please let him enjoy the ride, it's part of his treatment.'

The men shrugged and started on a game of football. Ophelia scanned the distance, but there was no sign of Clarence. Hoping she hadn't done the wrong thing in letting him dash off like that, she sat down to wait for him to come back.

When he returned, he looked just as he had when he'd tried to keep up with the motorcar taking Mama and George away. His cheeky grin hadn't changed; he was the Clarence of her dreams, here beside her, safe and well.

He came to a sudden stop and almost fell off the cycle. 'I remember I had a bicycle once, when I was younger. It was a long time ago.'

Ophelia would not let herself become downhearted. He remembered some things and was confused about others. She would stay confident of his recovery.

He had made an excellent start. 'Would you like to join in the game with the other soldiers?'

Clarence nodded, but stood on the sidelines, his vibrancy lost.

★　★　★

Ophelia was undecided about showing Clarence the letter. She knew the words off by heart and recited them in her head as she watched Clarence digging the vegetable patch. 'All is well here … you mustn't worry … I will survive … you would like the horses.' Physically, he was as robust as ever. His body appeared powerful, and his muscles looked strong as he gripped the gardening fork. She enjoyed watching as he dug into the dark soil and turned it over.

'Clarence, tell me about the horses.'

He paused and rested on the spade. 'At the Front? What do you know?'

'In a letter, you said I'd like them.'

'Did I write to you?'

'You did. I was delighted to hear you

were safe.'

'I felt sorry for the horses. It was a hard life for them, and many were injured and killed. What a waste the war is. Death and destruction.' He gazed into the distance and suddenly flinched. Ophelia rushed over and put her arms round him.

'What happened?' she asked.

'I was back fighting. There was an explosion.' Clarence was breathing heavily.

'You're safe now, here with me and Beaumont, the people who love you.'

'Yes, thank you.' He looked into her eyes. 'You are beautiful. Your eyes are brown like chestnuts.' He gently twisted a handful of her hair. 'Dark with a hint of red.'

Ophelia pulled away. 'Let us walk, Clarence, and I'll read what you wrote to me. Listen.' They walked together along the path which led to the greenhouses. '*My dearest Ophelia, I hope you are in good health and Beaumont too ...*'

By the time she read, '*Much love, Clarence,*' tears were streaming down his face.

'I am starting to remember how I felt when I wrote that letter. I was homesick. I missed you and Beaumont almost more than I could stand.' He paused. 'I recollect what I should have told you before I left.'

'That's good.' Ophelia wasn't certain it *was* good. She had wanted his memory to return, but knew what he was about to say. She'd known from the moment she'd first read his letter. Rejecting him would break her heart, but she must.

'What I should have said was that I love you. I've loved you for a long time and I want to marry you.' He flung himself down on his knees. 'Ophelia, will you marry me?' he said.

And then he jumped up again. 'I must ask Beaumont first. I am sorry, Ophelia, I have made a mess of things, but he will agree I am sure.'

'Stop, stop! You must not say anything to Papa. I have told you, I am engaged to a man called Lemuel. He is a good man. It is all arranged. When the war ends, we will be married. I am sorry, Clarence.'

Clarence stared at her for a long moment before saying, 'Then I might as well go back to the Front now.'

In spite of Ophelia's entreaties that they should go back to the house together, Clarence walked off in the opposite direction.

Furious with herself for complicating things even further, Ophelia went to the mill, wanting to take her mind off her swirling emotions. She opened the door of the office and was pleased to find her father there. 'Papa, I have come to see if I may be of use here.'

Beaumont turned and smiled at his daughter. 'It's always a pleasure to see you, my dear. You seem to spend all your time with Clarence. How is he progressing?'

'Oh, Papa,' she sighed, 'I think I have made him ill again.'

'Nonsense, you could never do that. You are wonderful company. Perhaps you both need a little time apart from each other. I have a job here you could do.' He pushed a bundle of papers towards her. 'If you can sort these into any semblance of order, it would help enormously. Now, I have to leave and check on the cloth being dispatched.'

Unsure whether her father had invented the task to keep her mind busy or not, Ophelia started to sift through the papers, putting them into piles. When she had finished, she sat back in the chair, feeling more relaxed. As far as Clarence was concerned, she could do no more; she had told him about Lemuel, and that must be the end of the matter. And if he returned to the war? That was what most of the young men at the hospital did, and she must accept it.

⋆　⋆　⋆

Ophelia saw little of Clarence over the next few days. She hoped he was all right, but she did not seek him out, preferring instead to spend time at the mill with her father and Edna. They were very busy and needed all the hands available. Papa was spending more time supervising the workers, and he was certainly good for morale these days. He had smartened up his appearance, and his eyes were bright as he toured the building. Faith was his constant companion, and she seemed to bring him joy, something Ophelia wished for Clarence.

Taking a break from doing the accounts, Ophelia went to the mill library. She found it comforting to be there. As she browsed the shelves, she automatically tidied the books. Glancing at the titles, she saw a name which made her giddy: Hope Beaumont! It was her dear mama's book, the first one she'd had published after their marriage: a travelogue which she'd written on her honeymoon in Paris.

Putting it to one side, she quickly returned the rest of the books to the shelf, picked up her mama's book, and left the library. Darting to the office, she threw on her cloak and headed for the moor, wanting peace and tranquillity in which to read her mother's words.

From a window at the mill, Beaumont watched his daughter scurrying away towards the moor. He could imagine her torment; her beloved Clarence was not well, and his behaviour towards her was difficult to cope with. However, she was engaged to be married to Lemuel. Beaumont considered this. Lemuel himself was a likeable sort of man, although there was no spark about him as far as Beaumont could tell. The fact that he was James Henderson's son influenced his perspective, but that was not fair of him.

Perhaps it was time for him to intervene. 'Faith, come on, girl,' he called.

The dog scrambled to her feet at the sound of her master's voice and walked at his side. He left by the back door of the mill and shivered in the frigid air outside. He walked purposefully towards the house, knowing it was approaching luncheon time.

His luck was in. 'Clarence,' he called, 'how good to see you. Are you well

305

today?' Immediately, he knew it was a silly question, as Clarence looked pale and dishevelled and wouldn't look Beaumont in the eye. 'Shall we go into the house? It's cold out here, and Faith is freezing, look at her.'

At the sound of her name, Faith looked up at the two men. Then she gently nuzzled Clarence's hand with her nose. At first, it was as though he hadn't noticed, and then Clarence bent down and took her face in his hands, smiling at her. 'Is this the same dog we chose for you, Beaumont? She has grown, but she has the same lively nature.'

'She has been a lifesaver, dear boy. I was wondering if you would look after her for me for a few days. I am particularly busy at the mill, and she needs more attention than I can give her.'

Clarence said, 'What about Ophelia? Couldn't she take care of the dog?'

'She is helping out at the mill as well; we have a lot of work to do. If you can't see to Faith, it doesn't matter.' Quickly, Beaumont walked towards the house, and

Faith looked between the two of them, before sitting firmly at Clarence's feet. Aware that Clarence couldn't see his expression, Beaumont smiled.

Beaumont couldn't face food while his thoughts were on Ophelia. He gathered a thick coat and walked over the moor following the route he knew she would have taken. The bracken path was damp and he stumbled his way along it until he heard the sound of weeping. His heart constricted and his eyes became moist.

'I'm here, my darling child,' he called, hurrying to her side. He put his arms around her and let her cry into him until she was spent. Then the two huddled together until Ophelia felt in a pocket for her handkerchief and wiped her nose. 'I have Mama's book here. Do you remember it?' She held it out for her papa to see.

He took it from her and traced the author's name with his index finger, a touch so light it could have been a feather. 'Yes, I remember it.'

'Papa, I am so lonely without her and George,' Ophelia sniffed.

'So am I, darling, so am I.'

'And I miss Clarence, the Clarence I knew. Now he hardly speaks to me. He hates me, I know.'

'That can't be true. How could anyone hate you?' He pulled her to her feet. 'We must go back, it's too cold to be out, you will catch a chill.'

'Then you would have to take care of me,' replied Ophelia, a small smile on her lips.

'Me? I'm *much* too busy to do that.' He caught her hand and kissed it.

Nearing the house, he heard Faith barking, and he pointed. 'Look, Ophelia, Faith and Clarence are playing. Shall we join them?'

But she shook her head and veered off towards the mill. 'I've got the accounts to work on, and don't forget you have an appointment later.'

When she was out of sight, Beaumont went over to Clarence. 'We need to talk, young man. Come into the house.' He walked off, relieved to hear Clarence and Faith behind him.

Back in the warm house, Beaumont asked, 'Clarence, what are your feelings for Ophelia? I must know the truth.'

The younger man sank into a chair and put his head in his hands. 'The truth? It is that I love her; it seems as if that was always so. But she has told me she loves another.'

'She is engaged to be married to another, but it is you she loves, Clarence. I give you my word.'

★   ★   ★

The atmosphere in the family's part of the house was heavy with gloom. Mealtimes were mainly silent despite Beaumont's efforts to lighten the mood. He noticed Clarence staring at Ophelia. He knew she was immensely sad, but she worked herself to exhaustion every day. She had told him this enabled her to sleep at night without thoughts of Clarence tormenting her. He could hardly bear the unhappiness of these two young people.

'Good morning, Ophelia, there is a

letter for you.' Beaumont handed her an envelope as she took her place at the breakfast table. 'What will you be doing today, Clarence?'

'I thought I would take Faith for a long walk and then work in the garden.'

'Are your dizzy spells decreasing yet?' Beaumont tried not to worry about Clarence being alone on the long walks he had started to take, as he had confidence in Faith. He was sure she would come home for help in an emergency. She had an instinct for knowing who was most in need of her companionship, even sleeping in Clarence's room at night.

'No, they are as bad as ever. I am unlikely to be allowed to go back to the Front just yet. More's the pity.'

'I, for one, am glad of that, and I'm sure I am not alone. Although I would not wish you to be unwell.' Beaumont looked at Ophelia, who was engrossed in the letter she had received.

'Papa, Clarence, I have received a letter from Lemuel's father. Listen to this.' She scanned the sheet, biting her lip as if undecided about something. '*I am sorry to be the one to impart bad news ... Lemuel is to marry someone more suitable ... she is charming ... from an aristocratic family ... they are to be married shortly ... in time you too will find a suitable match ... Lemuel and I wish you well.*' Ophelia rested her head in her hands.

'My dear girl, are you quite all right?' He was relieved when she looked up and grinned

'Oh, Papa, I am better than all right. I am ecstatic. It is as though a huge weight has been lifted, and I am free. I am free!' She stood up and spun round the room, finally stopping behind Clarence's chair.

Beaumont knew he should leave the young people to themselves, but he wanted to witness Clarence's reaction to what he was sure Ophelia was about to say. And, Ophelia being Ophelia, she came straight out with it.

'I love you, Clarence,' she said, resting her hands on his shoulders. 'I knew I loved you years ago, but circumstances caused me to remain silent. When you declared *your* love for *me*, I didn't know how to explain everything. Now, with Lemuel out of the way, everything is easy. Will you marry me, Clarence?'

Beaumont chuckled. He should probably be challenging James or Lemuel Henderson to a duel, or whatever one did when one's daughter was jilted, but his heart was dancing and all he could feel was a tremendous happiness. He knew he had no place here, and silently left the room.

★　★　★

'You haven't lost your impetuousness, have you?' Clarence said, shaking his head as he stood and turned to face her.

'Would you want me to?' she countered, feeling flirtatious.

'Ophelia, are you sure it's me you want to marry? It's a bit of a sudden change of mind on your behalf, isn't it? Engaged to be married to someone, get rejected before you've got to the altar, and then pick me to be your husband.' Clarence frowned at her.

Ophelia felt a panic building inside her. What Clarence said was true from a certain perspective, but she wished he knew how much she had pined for him while he was away. Perhaps she shouldn't have asked for Clarence's hand in marriage — or, at least, not immediately after having divulged the contents of the letter which, as he had quite correctly pointed out, rejected her. She should curb her hot-headedness which had been inherited from her mama. How was she to convince Clarence of her love?

She placed a hand lightly on his arm and said, 'I understand how this could appear to you, but the truth is that I have loved you and craved your return, and also your love, for what seems like a lifetime.' Clarence turned his head away and Ophelia felt a touch as cold as marble skitter down her spine. 'Have I lost you, Clarence?' she whispered. The next thing she knew, she was fighting for her breath as she was muffled against his chest. She couldn't hear the words he was saying, but he was holding her tightly and stroking her hair, making her feel dizzy.

'Dearest Ophelia. I had to hear it from your own sweet lips. Although I did have forewarning that it might be as you say.'

'Papa? It was he who told you of my feelings, wasn't it?' She should have guessed that Papa would help her when she needed him most. And then, all thoughts of him vanished as Clarence's lips were upon hers. After what could have been a few seconds or a whole lifetime, they gently pulled apart.

Clarence took Ophelia's arm, leading her from the room. 'We must find Beaumont. You should thank him for finding you such a good husband.'

'You are not my husband yet,' teased Ophelia, good-naturedly. 'But I shall get used to the idea — eventually.' She laughed, brushed herself free from him, and ran along the hallway with Clarence close on her heels.

'What's this?' asked Beaumont, his eyebrows raised. 'Am I to take it that your high spirits are due to young love?'

'Indeed, Beaumont,' smiled Clarence, slowing as he approached him. 'I should like to ask for your blessing. We wish to be married soon.'

Ophelia felt a wave of joy wash through her as she put her arms around the two people she loved most in the world.

'Take her,' laughed Beaumont. 'And get her to the altar as quickly as you can. She needs a firm hand, just like her mother!' Then his face grew serious. 'If you two have half the happiness Hope and I shared, you will be truly blessed.'

We do hope that you have enjoyed reading this large print book.

Did you know that all of our titles are available for purchase?

We publish a wide range of high quality large print books including:
Romances, Mysteries, Classics
General Fiction
Non Fiction and Westerns

Special interest titles available in large print are:
The Little Oxford Dictionary
Music Book, Song Book
Hymn Book, Service Book

Also available from us courtesy of Oxford University Press:
Young Readers' Dictionary
(large print edition)
Young Readers' Thesaurus
(large print edition)

For further information or a free brochure, please contact us at:
Ulverscroft Large Print Books Ltd.,
The Green, Bradgate Road, Anstey,
Leicester, LE7 7FU, England.
Tel: (00 44) **0116 236 4325**
Fax: (00 44) **0116 234 0205**

AN UNEXPECTED LOVE

Angela Britnell

Kieran O'Neill, a Nashville song-writer, is in Cornwall, sorting through his late Great-Uncle Peter's house. Since being betrayed by Helen, his former girlfriend and cowriter, falling in love has been the last thing on his mind . . . Sandi Thomas, a struggling single mother, has put aside her own artistic dreams — and any chance of a personal life — to concentrate on raising her son, Pip. But as feelings begin to grow between Kieran and Sandi, might they finally become the family they've both been searching for?

PALACE OF DECEPTION

Helena Fairfax

When a Mediterranean princess disappears with just weeks to go before her investiture, Lizzie Smith takes on the acting role of her life — she is to impersonate Princess Charlotte so that the ceremony can go ahead. As Lizzie immerses herself in preparation, her only confidante is Léon, her quiet bodyguard. In the glamorous setting of the Palace of Montverrier, Lizzie begins to fall for Léon. But what secrets is he keeping from her? And who can she really trust?

SHADOWS AT BOWERLY HALL

Carol MacLean

Forced to work as a governess after the death of her father, Amelia Thorne travels north to Yorkshire and the isolated Bowerly Hall. Charles, Viscount Bowerly, is a darkly brooding employer, and Amelia is soon convinced that the stately home hold secrets and danger in its shadows. Then a spate of burglaries in the county raises tensions amongst the villagers and servants, and Amelia finds herself on the hunt for the culprit. Can Charles be trusted?

SUMMER'S DREAM

Jean M. Long

Talented designer Juliet Croft is devastated when the company she works for closes. She takes a temporary job at the Linden Manor Hotel, but soon hears rumours that the business is in financial difficulties — and suspects that Sheldon's, a rival company, is involved. During her work, she renews her friendship with Scott, a former colleague. At the same time, she must cope with her growing feelings for Martin Glover, the hotel manager. Trouble is, he's already taken . . .

SEEING SHADOWS

Susan Udy

Lexie Brookes is busy running her hairdressing salon and wondering what to do about her cooling relationship with her partner, Danny. When the jewellery shop next door is broken into via her own premises, the owner — the wealthy and infuriatingly arrogant Bruno Cavendish — blames her for his losses. Then Danny disappears, and Lexie is suddenly targeted by a mysterious stalker. To add to the turmoil, Bruno appears to be attracted to her, and she finds herself equally drawn to him . . .

A DATE WITH ROMANCE

Toni Anders

Refusing to live in the shadow of her father, a famous TV chef, Lauren Tate runs her own cake shop with her best friend, Daisy. Having been unlucky in love, Lauren pours her energy into her business — until she meets her handsome new neighbour, Jake, who is keen to strike up a friendship with her. Will Lauren decide to take him up on the offer? Then Daisy has an accident, and announces she'll be following her partner to America once she has healed — leaving Lauren with some difficult choices . . .